I0722475

Aerobics Can Be Deadly

Bucket List Mysteries 1

Ryan Rivers

Copyright @ 2022 Ryan Rivers

All rights reserved. No part of this book may be reproduced in any form or by any electronic or mechanical means, including information storage and retrieval systems, without permission in writing from the publisher, except by reviewers, who may quote brief passages in a review.
ISBN: 978-1-956244-03-8 (Paperback Edition)

Characters and events in this book are fictitious. Any similarity to real persons, living or dead, is coincidental and not intended by the author.

Cover by Dominik Schwaeger
www.dominikschwaeger.de

Printed and bound in the USA
Published by Partners in Crime Press LLC
320 Gold Ave SW Ste 620 PMD 2041
Albuquerque, NM 87102

Visit www.ryanriversbooks.com

Acknowledgments

I WOULD LIKE TO ACKNOWLEDGE the individuals whose expertise and support made this book a reality.

My designer, Dominik Schwaeger, brings life to Bluebonnet
Hills and its quirky residents. I'm grateful for his artistic bril-
liance, patience, and sense of humor.

Thank you to my editor, Elizabeth A. White, whose skill has
elevated my storytelling. Your perceptiveness has helped me push
away my inner critic and trust my intuition.

Linda, Rashida, and Suzy also provided invaluable feedback
on the early (and multiple!) drafts.

Thanks also to Captain Edward Black, Taylor Triece (RN),

and Dr. DP Lyle for their expertise on police procedure, medicine, and forensics, respectively. While I worked to get my technical details accurate, any errors are mine.

I also want to acknowledge Dr. Ann, Crystal, Andrew, and Charles. Your expertise and experience helped me relay Sho and Levi's backstories with awareness and dignity.

I'm also grateful for the friendships I've developed with other writers. Thanks to Jacob for keeping me accountable. Thanks to Linda for never keeping me accountable. Your next brisket sandwich is on me (the coupon is in the mail, I swear).

Finally, to my son, who amazes me every day. It's a privilege to watch you grow and learn. I love you with my whole heart.

Chapter 1

I STUDIED THE BUCKET my sister, Jenny, placed in front of me.

"Draw, Sho-chan," she said, using my nickname.

All around the bucket, cranes glided above turtle nests. Both animals represented good health and longevity in Japanese culture, but my sister's artwork only gave the ridiculous bucket-list ceremony more pomp and circumstance.

"Explain the rules again," I said.

"There are no *rules*." Jenny had mastered the verbal eye roll. "You draw a piece of paper, read it, and do what it says. Don't overthink it."

I inspected the colorful confetti of paper inside. "What's the significance of your color-coded classification system?"

"My color-coded…? Are you asking what the different colors mean?"

"My bucket list wasn't that long." Levi Blue, town mayor and former star of the detective show *Tween of the Crime*, hung from an inversion table while gripping a spare rib, which wasn't the oddest thing he'd done that day.

We sat in the parlor of the six-thousand-square-foot Texas McMansion he'd converted into a fan museum.

"Your list was a little thin," Jenny said, "so I added some ideas. Just a pinch of spice. I wrote mine on the pink paper."

A pinch? The pink papers resembled a bouquet of cherry blossoms. "What color are my ideas?"

Jenny averted her gaze. "Yellow, I think?"

I sifted through the papers. "There're only two, maybe three, yellow papers here. I offered practical, evidence-based suggestions."

"This isn't a life plan, Sho-chan. A bucket list is the ultimate list of big-ticket items. Shockingly, 'Diversify my stock portfolio' doesn't fit that definition. Your ideas were a bit… dry."

"Dry?"

"Okay, boring."

"Big-ticket items don't fund themselves." I returned the bucket to the coffee table with more force than I'd intended. "Smart saving includes a healthy mix of stocks, bonds, and mutual funds. And spare me the nonsense on annuities."

Jenny sighed. "Thank you for making my point."

"What's on your list, little sister?" I folded my arms and leaned back against the couch Levi had upholstered with images of his former tween likeness. "You dropped out of an expensive culinary school to move to small-town Texas and open a café. What's left to conquer?"

"All strategic decisions, and let's not fight. I'm too busy to remove bloodstains from Levi's couch. And I have lots of things on my list: kayaking down the Nile, off-roading through Death Valley, visiting Machu Picchu before it's gone, flying into a volcano, and bathing in its hot springs while it's erupting…"

"I was with you until the lava bath," Levi said through a mouthful of rib. "Those sound exciting, Jen, but not the experiences I wanted."

"Everything you put on your list is here. You're the green paper." She sat in the wingback across from me and fluffed a Levi-shaped pillow. "Only your items were… too normal, too everyday. I mean, host a traditional Thanksgiving dinner? Go to a prom? Those are sweet, Levi, really, but no thirty-something guy goes to a prom. Jail time is not an experience you want."

"I know it's silly, but those *are* my big-ticket items. All my Thanksgivings and dances were filmed in front of a live studio audience."

"Your items also fit the definition of a *bucket list*," I said. "The denotation includes nothing about 'big-ticket items.' It's simply a list of things you want to do before dying."

"Denotation?" Jenny sighed.

"Pardon me for consulting a dictionary."

Jenny used her foot to nudge the bucket closer. "Draw."

"Why am I the one drawing?" I asked Levi. "This is your bucket list, not mine."

"Your hands are cleaner, so I'm calling in my understudy." He wiggled his sauce-stained fingers before taking another bite of rib. "These are delicious, Jen. Put these on your menu, for sure."

I placed my hand in the bucket and flicked through the papers. "Let me try to find one of Levi's. His are green, you said?"

Jenny stood and raised the bucket above my head. "You don't pick a color. That's not how it works."

"Hmm, so there *are* rules?" I raised my arm and flopped my

hand inside the bucket, swirling the papers for dramatic effect that impressed no one. I unfolded the paper—pink, of course—and read, "Do a triathlon."

"Ooh, the race of endurance." Jenny clasped her hands and wore the swoony expression she usually reserved for Jane Austen novels. "Running, swimming, cycling. That's a great first experience to check off your bucket list, Levi."

Levi chewed that over by gnawing on his rib. "Meh. Pass. Pick something else, Tanaka-san."

I raised my hand to draw, but Jenny smacked it away.

"You can't pass! Those aren't the rules."

"More rules!" I rubbed the sting from my hand.

"The paper says triathlon, so do a triathlon." Jenny sat back down, her arms wrapped around the bucket.

"You don't *do* a triathlon," I said. "Athletes train for months, oftentimes longer."

"Then train." Jenny shrugged. "A bucket list has no deadline."

"Actually, it does."

"Triathlon," Levi repeated. "Doesn't feel very bucket list-y. Feels like work and effort."

"Think of this as a rebirth," Jenny said. "You're starting your bucket list by running away from your problems and toward something better."

"You don't need a bucket list to avoid your problems." I slapped my thighs. "Tackle them head-on. That's what I do."

"Is that what you've been doing in my spare room for six weeks?" Jenny asked, amused. "I wondered what you were doing between brooding and sulking."

Six weeks? I guessed time flew when you were escaping your responsibilities and detoxing from a prescription-drug dependency.

Attempting to regain control of the conversation, I said, "Bucket list aside, Levi, you committed to more exercise and a better diet. Hanging like a bat while spewing rib meat doesn't fulfill that commitment."

"*Au contraire*, Tanaka-san. The infomercial host said an inversion table would improve my blood flow and circulation, keeping me well-stretched and lanky."

"Uh-huh."

"I need to maintain limberness for situations requiring physical comedy."

"You're the mayor," I said. "Zero situations require physical comedy."

"Slapstick would vastly improve our council meetings. Imagine Barbara Lou Sinclair taking a custard pie to the face. She'd be tolerable. Almost." He shook his half-eaten rib at me. "As for diet, meat is an essential part of my food pyramid. I read all about it."

"You read? A book?"

"Don't be irrational. I read the captions of a video on my social media feed. It's the Caveman Diet. Meat, fish, eggs. That's it. If it was good enough for my primitive ancestors, it's good enough for me."

"A diet high in fat, cholesterol, and sodium. A solid plan if your target life expectancy is thirty-five."

"I just follow the science."

"I've created a nutritional program for you," I said. "Many of the patients I cared for in the ICU got their nutrition from an IV bag. You're well on your way with this Fred Flintstone diet."

"Hold on, boys. I'm getting an idea." Jenny tapped her temple.

"Run, Levi. Run as far as those lanky legs will take you."

My sister perched on the edge of her seat. "Levi would be more likely to complete a triathlon—and enjoy the process—if he trained with a buddy. Some accountability."

"Now there's an idea." Levi's rock-star lips puckered as he contemplated.

"Am I the alleged buddy in this scenario?" I scratched my

fingers across Levi's couch. "Investing in a gym membership seems impractical. I'm only visiting."

"The Lone Star Gym has all-new equipment, personal training, group exercise... and month-to-month contracts." Jenny snuggled into the wingback with a smile.

"No excuses, Tanaka-san." The inversion table squeaked when Levi raised his arms to maneuver himself upright. "You committed, too, remember? To take more risks, to loosen the top button of your shirt."

"I made that commitment while zip-tied to a chair, about to be buried alive in concrete."

"Always with the theatrics." Levi released the inversion table's handle and swatted rib bits off his jeans. "You've already taken the first big step: acknowledging you're a curmudgeonly grumpy pants—"

"Grumpy pants?"

"Who plans every detail with snooze-inducing precision while skulking around in dumpy, schlumpy monochromatic clothes."

"The label calls this oatmeal." I hugged myself to conceal the pullover. "Neutrals are classic. I do not skulk, nor have I described myself as—"

"Tanaka-san, you can stand there lecturing me, in your fifty shades of beige, or you can embrace a healthier lifestyle."

I looked at the jelly roll forming around my dumpy, schlumpy monochromatic midsection. Most of my nausea and headaches—perks from detoxing—had subsided, but the thought of clinging to a treadmill made my skin prickle. Still, a hit of endorphins would do me good. "I suppose a tour of the gym's facilities wouldn't hurt."

"Eureka! I'll check the charge on the Segways." Levi staggered into the hallway, dizzy from the inversion therapy or going for physical comedy. "Don't forget your helmet."

"Wait." But he was gone, so I glared at the life-size cardboard cutout of Levi holding his Tween Choice Award for Best Bedhead. "He played me again."

"And you're still always surprised." Jenny released her grip on the bucket and produced a Hello Kitty helmet from behind the wingback. "Figured you'd need this."

My lip curled at the mouthless cat wearing a big red bow, and I pointed at the cutout. "Let's swap me with Cardboard Levi. Truly, no one in town would think twice."

"Please, Sho-chan. You're more important to Levi than cardboard." Jenny grinned. "Never forget—you're oatmeal."

Chapter 2

THE STARK-WHITE EXTERIOR of the Lone Star gleamed in the late-afternoon sun. Levi and I steered our Segways around rows of cars into parking spaces reserved for motorcycles and other smaller transportation modes.

"You okay?" In one fluid motion, Levi stepped off the Segway and unsnapped his helmet. "I've avoided this place since…"

"Since we almost died here?" Unlike Levi, I tripped off my Segway and poked myself in the mouth, grappling for the helmet snap.

Levi used the toe of his boot to point at the ground. "My big, beautiful bust would've gone right here."

Six weeks ago, the parking lot had been a construction site for Levi's TV fan museum, complete with a bronze bust capturing his tween glory days.

"Instead, we found a wall of cash and two dead bodies. They've paved over tragedy and put up a parking lot." I shook my head to scatter those memories. "Before we go in, perhaps we should discuss a strategy."

Levi's lips plumped with confusion. "That doesn't sound like me."

"Agreed. But gym memberships get expensive." We moved toward the front door, past the newly planted shrubs and flowers that needed time to grow into their new homes. "Sure, they may offer a low monthly membership, but you have to consider all the additional costs for perks. That's where they get you. We want to be perk free."

Levi raised his eyebrows. "What sort of perks?"

"Pressed juice, sauna access, extra towels, Zumba classes… things like that. What's your budget?"

"What's this Zumba you speak of?"

"You've lost my point." I squinted and used my hand to block the sun. "It's a fitness class with Latin music. You do moves like the salsa and the samba."

"*Ole!*" Levi snapped his fingers. "Add that to our perk list."

"That's the opposite of a budget." I opened the door and received a spritzing of chemical cleaner.

"Looks like somebody spilled their oatmeal," Levi quipped, pointing at the splatters on my pullover.

"Yikes! My bad, sir." A teenager pressed a rag against my chest with his rubber-gloved hand. His furious blotting caused me to stumble back into Levi.

When the young man looked up, a smile emerged. "Hi, Mayor Blue. Super sorry I doused your budget officer. I was cleaning fingerprints off the glass."

Budget officer?

"Trevor, my man." Levi returned the smile. "How's the new job treating you?"

"Everyone here is super nice, and the hours are super flexible." Trevor absently blotted me as he spoke. "Ms. Ramona lets me lift after my shifts. Thanks again for your recommendation."

Sufficiently blotted, I sidestepped Trevor and his rag. "We're looking for some membership information. Do you have an itemized list of fees and a sample contract we could review?"

"We're doing a triathlon," Levi added.

Trevor tilted his head toward the front desk. "Ms. Ramona can help with all that. She's super nice."

Super.

"You helped him get a job?" I asked Levi as we followed Trevor.

Levi shrugged. "When I created the backstory for this mayor role, I chose 'vibrant economy' as one of my character motivations." He stopped with a theatrical jerk, raised his head, and sniffed the air—again, not the oddest thing he'd done that day. "What's that smell?"

I looked at my stained clothing. "That cleaner has lavender in it. Perhaps some citrus too?"

Levi inhaled deeply, his nostrils flaring. "That's not citrus. Why, it's ripe opportunity."

I sniffed my pullover. "That might be vanilla."

Trevor set his spray bottle on the front desk. "Ms. Ramona? Mayor Blue and his budget officer want to join the Lone Star."

"I'm not his budget officer."

"Oh, double yikes." Trevor stiffened. "His… financial adviser? You just seem so… so…"

"Beige?" Levi offered.

Trevor swallowed a laugh. "Official."

Ramona clapped, bringing us to attention. "Mayor Blue,

welcome, welcome. We're honored you've visited us today." She giggled and adjusted the shoulders of her white polo. "I'm Ramona Sinclair, club manager and married to the co-owner." She extended her hand to both of us.

I accepted the handshake and smiled. "I was just asking Trevor about your prices—"

"Oh, I bet you want a tour."

"No, prices—"

Ramona released a laugh that bordered on hysterical. Her lips pulled into a grin as she nodded to music that only she heard. "Oh, I see how it is. *You're* the funny one. I've got my eye on you!"

Levi's eyes narrowed. "Tanaka-san is never the funny one."

"Boo, dollars and cents." Ramona cocked her head and released a snore loud enough to startle the people on the nearby treadmills. "Snooze-a-roonie. Am I right, or am I right?"

I'd never met anyone more wrong.

"Finally, someone who speaks my language," Levi said.

Locking on her target, Ramona slipped around the desk and grabbed Levi's shoulder. "Lemme show you boys around. We find new members want to experience the value they'll receive from being an elite member of the Lone Star. You want that, too, right?"

Levi nodded compliantly. "Don't forget the perks. We want all the perks."

Ramona lifted her magic fingers from Levi's shoulders. "We've got special discounts for dapper mayors and his rascally staff. Wink, wink."

She launched into a well-rehearsed walk and talk, so we had to jog to keep up. "We have five main areas in the gym: stretching and mobility, cardio, functional fitness, free weights, and team activities."

We moved into the cardio area, where Ramona spun around and walked backward, using her arms to motion to the ellipticals, treadmills, stationary bikes, and stair-climbers. "As y'all see, we spare no expense on equipment."

I stopped to observe the members: training, sweating, and striving toward some goal. Their faces held semipained expressions, but they glowed from perseverance. The whirrs and swooshes from their machines created an interwoven melody of achievement. It looked exhausting.

My eyes landed on a polished-steel-framed stair-climber at least eight feet tall. The climber perched at the top watched over everyone with cool indifference. My throat constricted, and I gasped from holding my breath. How I craved that indifference, that enhanced focus to keep stepping, to keep striving.

I had ambition—once.

"Everything's bigger at the Lone Star." Ramona vise-gripped my shoulders as she cooed into my ear. "You step on that three times a week, and your calves will bulge into hunky li'l baseballs in no time."

Hunky li'l baseball calves didn't make my top-ten list of fitness goals. Yet, perhaps joining a gym wasn't such an impractical idea—no more red wine every night, better sleep, early-morning climbs, and a less lethargic existence.

"Is that a studio?" Levi pointed toward the far end of the gym.

Ramona released her hold and strode toward the glass-enclosed room. "That's the Rodeo Room, the larger of our two studios. We hold most of our group exercise classes here—Pilates, yoga, Zumba, and aerobics, of course. Y'all know my sister-in-law is an internationally recognized aerobics queen."

Levi gagged, an involuntary response to any mention of Barbara Lou Sinclair. She'd engaged Levi in some savvy negotiations over the abandoned fan museum lot, arguing the discovery of two dead bodies depreciated its value, which was a fair point.

"Excuse the mess in there," Ramona said. "The studio doubles as our production studio, and we're shooting another aerobics workout tomorrow."

"A shoot!" Levi's eyes widened. Ramona had said the magic word.

"This'll be Barbie's thirty-seventh video and her seventh with Nick Batista."

"A shoot!" Levi repeated. "Do you have any available parts? I'll work for scale."

Ramona gave a killer-clown smile. "Oh, of course. You were in that kid detective show."

"Tween," Levi said. "Tween detective show."

"*Tween* detective show." Ramona bopped her forehead with her palm. "Earth to Ramona!" Another one of her nearly hysterical brays ripped through the gym, bouncing off the walls somewhere between the kettlebells and the squat bars. "I forgot you used to be an actor."

Levi's face drooped as he absorbed the comment. "Used to be."

Ramona's jaw dropped when she realized her comment had released her hold on Levi's wallet. "It's… It's just that you're such a fantastic mayor that I forget how versatile and natural you are."

I stepped in front of Levi before he blinked dollar signs. "We're not interested in group exercise. That's an additional cost, I presume?"

Ramona aimed that smile at me. "What exactly are your fitness goals, Mr. Tanaka?"

"Training for a triathlon."

"Wonderful." She clapped. "You're right. Group exercise wouldn't help y'all."

I flashed Levi my smug toldja-so expression. Wink, wink, indeed.

"You boys need a trainer."

Wait. What?

"Nick is an excellent trainer," Ramona said. "And he trains teams…" Her eyes drifted to me. "Of all fitness levels."

I stood straighter and sucked in my stomach. "We're only gathering information today. Pricing information."

Defeated, Ramona let her smile curl into a sneer. "I can get you what you need." She bolted between me and Levi and toward the front desk.

Levi raised a hand to the glass-enclosed studio. "I'd never considered starring in fitness videos."

"Perhaps because you lack fitness experience."

"Why would that stop me? Do you think those productions have character arcs, plot twists, and physical comedy?"

"Your lunging around in spandex would qualify as comedy, yes." I directed Levi back to the front desk. "Now, let me do the talking. Ramona has some weird hold over you. I'm afraid you'll walk out of here with a second mortgage."

Levi raised his nose in the air and inhaled deeply, thumping his fists against his chest. "There's that smell again." He spun around in circles and continued sniffing.

Ramona fanned several pieces of paper in front of me, turning each around for me to read. "These are our most updated prices and fees."

I pulled the price sheet closer to my face and wrinkled my brow. "Yikes. Is this the annual fee?"

"Monthly but before the discounts."

"And the added costs of the training," I muttered.

"Don't forget the perks!" Levi grasped the edge of the desk, apparently dizzy from scent chasing.

"Consider the value, Mr. Tanaka." Ramona seemed recovered from her earlier defeat. "Nick is a certified trainer. He trains with you here, plans your meals, performs unscheduled accountability check-ins—"

"Unscheduled?"

Ramona nodded with bobblehead precision. "He wants you to follow the plan. He might pop into your work one morning, just to check on you."

The thought of anyone popping anywhere in my vicinity annoyed me. Of course, I had no job for anyone to pop into, adding to my annoyance.

The front door sprang open, sending the price sheet sailing through the air. I grabbed for it, nearly poking Ramona in the eye.

She slipped and rolled like a boxer and faced the door. "Perfect timing. Here's our star trainer now."

Nick Batista leaned against the doorframe, mesmerized by his phone. He caught the closing door with the toe of his shoe, kicking it back far enough to move out of its path.

Ramona waved. "Nicky, there are some new members I'd like you to meet."

He continued to stare at his phone, adjusting one of his earbuds. Then he snorted and glanced around the gym as if everyone were in on the joke. His eyes flicked to Ramona, whom he jutted his chin toward in greeting.

Ramona giggled, a welcome sound after the hyena-inspired laughs she'd subjected us to earlier. "We have some new members who need your help, Nicky. I'm sure you recognize Mayor Blue."

Nick's attention landed on Levi, whom he assessed as if he were a zoo animal. He nodded and glanced at me, starting at my head and landing on my gut. He sucked air through his teeth and removed an earbud. "'Sup?"

Chapter 3

N ICK REMOVED HIS OTHER EARBUD and spun it on the desk. "The mayor and his staff are training for a triathlon," Ramona said. "Give them a quick consult—a little taste of what you can offer." Her voice had suddenly gone husky.

"Romy." Nick's charming smile revealed a mouthful of pearly white teeth that I inexplicably wanted to punch. "How do you expect to make money when you keep giving it away?"

"It's customer relations, Nicky." Ramona's tongue flicked over her top lip.

I raised my arm to signal we were still in the room.

Nick propped his elbow on the desk and used it to pivot toward us. "Hey! Annie!" He barked.

"No, I'm Sho—"

Nick held his hand in front of my face and stepped between me and Levi. "Annie!"

I turned but found no redheaded orphan singing about tomorrow, only Trevor with a caddy of cleaning supplies.

"You do what I ask?" Nick said.

Trevor gave a thumbs-up. "Yes, sir, Mr. Nick. Everything's in your locker. I also stopped by your place and took a steak out of the freezer. It'll be ready to cook when you want it."

"You're an okay orphan, Annie." Nick placed the earbuds in their case and snapped the lid shut. "Grab me some water while I entertain these guys. You know the kind I like."

Trevor surveyed the sweaty cardio equipment, which needed a wipe down, before squaring his shoulders. "Sure thing, Mr. Nick. I replaced the filter this morning. Water should be cold by now."

"I can blend you a smoothie, Nicky." Ramona folded herself across the desk.

Nick chuckled. "I'll stick with the water. For my safety."

Ramona blanched and busied herself with stacking papers.

"Sorry about that, bro." Nick turned his attention to Levi. "I'm about to break my fast. When it's time to eat, I don't want to be waiting for my meal to defrost. You feel me?"

"Putting your body in starvation mode," I muttered. "That part of the demonstration?"

A muscle in Nick's jaw tensed. "You say something? What's your name again? Shoe?"

"Sho. Fasting isn't the smartest approach to nutrition. And you certainly don't break a fast with red meat."

"You a doctor or something, Shoe Sho?"

"Or something. Nurse."

"Nuuuuurse."

Nick's response was yawn-inducing compared to the other male-nurse mocking I'd endured.

"From the looks of it, you both need some training."

I straightened. "Pardon?"

"What do you weigh? One thirty-five, one forty?" Nick glanced at my stomach, which he thumped. "My bad. More like one fifty? No one would hesitate to confront you two."

"Excuse me." Levi puffed his chest. "A critic once wrote that I had the physique of young Jimmy Stewart."

Nick's lip curled into a smirk.

I patted Levi's shoulder. "I doubt even Mr. Smith would respond graciously to these insults."

Levi squinted. "Who's Mr. Smith?"

"Jimmy Stewart's character in *Mr. Smith Goes to Washington.*"

"The sausage guy was an actor?"

"Sausage guy? That's Jimmy Dean, not Jimmy Stewart!" Frustrated, I took a deep breath through my nose and blew it out in Nick's direction. "Look, compatibility is key to effective fitness training, and we don't respond to your, er, tactics." I looked at Ramona, who'd been watching the exchange. "We'll find somewhere else to train."

I stepped forward, causing Nick to make space for my exit. "Let's go," I said to Levi, who followed.

"Suit yourself," Nick replied when I grabbed the door handle. "Noodle Arms."

In the reflection in the glass door, I glared at Nick's mouthful of shark's teeth.

Levi stooped to my ear. "You going to take that, Noodle Arms?"

"Don't call me that."

"I'll give you two the bods and the confidence to confront anything life throws at you," Nick said. "Lemme show you some basic exercises. We can do some sparring."

Levi spun around. "Ooh, I love stage combat!"

I sighed in defeat.

"All right, Mr. Mayor, you're up first." Nick hopped from one foot to the other and punched the air. "You box?"

"Hand modeling is my backup career." Levi wiggled his fingers. "Can't risk the injury."

Nick's foot hopping ended with a stumble. "Uh, how about you, Florence Nightingale? You box? Or do you need smooth and dainty hands for sponge baths?"

I balled my hands into smooth and dainty fists and looked up again at my aloof hero, who lorded over the gym from his stair-climber.

"Catch." Nick tossed something that resembled two oversized cocktail olives speared by a foot-long toothpick.

I watched the contraption hit the ground and bounce off my loafers. "It's inflatable?"

From the equipment box, Nick removed two rubber platforms and tossed them onto the ground. "Push bumpers. Trains the upper body. Strengthens the core."

"Inflatable sparring?" I slipped off my loafers, walked onto a mat, and planted my feet on the platform that matched the color of my turquoise push bumper.

Nick tossed his bumper into the air with one hand and caught it with the other, then planted his feet on the opposite platform and relaxed into a slight squat. I mirrored his posture.

"The goal is to push each other off balance," he said.

Sure, Nick outweighed me by more than a hundred pounds, but it couldn't be that difficult. I used to do a lot of core exercises, and that conditioning didn't disappear overnight.

Whomp.

I stared up from the mat and massaged my tailbone. "What happened?"

"Guess you're unbalanced."

Stabbing the bumper into the mat, I pushed up and resumed my position.

"Sock it to him, Noodle Arms!" Levi, my traveling peanut gallery, yelled.

Nick lurched forward, but I blocked his bumper and pushed back.

"Nurse," he said when he'd recovered. "So, med school dropout?"

I blocked another attempt on my left and pushed forward, clenching my abdominals to stay upright. "That's not how nursing works. It's not a default career for—"

Whomp.

Nick raked a hand over his cropped black hair. "Sorry, Florence. You were saying?"

I sprang up and squatted deep into my platform. "What's your degree in? Nutrition? Exercise and sports science?"

Nick thrust his bumper at me. As I moved to block it, he switched positions. Using the balls of my feet, I pulled my body away from his, forcing him to stagger forward.

"I have some certifications, but mostly, I'm a graduate of the school of hard knocks."

"Are they accredited?"

Whomp.

Nick stood over me. "Ready to quit?"

Silently, I stood and reassumed my position.

"Your sister owns that café, right?" Nick blocked my move. "She single?"

"She doesn't date trainers," I lied, though I wasn't exactly sure. Jenny had once dated a sign spinner because she liked his fedora.

"That's cool. I just dumped my girl, so I'm down for a casual thing. I've seen her around town, mostly from behind, if you know what I mean. Your sister has got one fine—"

Whomp.

It took me a moment to realize I was standing. Nick blinked from the ground, absorbing the theory of gravity.

"Thanks for the demonstration." I dropped the push bumper, fully aware that was the closest I would ever get to a mic drop. Levi's dropped jaw only added to my enjoyment.

"Should I activate your membership cards?" Ramona gave a weary smile when I approached the front desk.

I saluted approval. Trevor, who'd returned with Nick's water bottle, tapped me on the shoulder.

"That was super cool, Mr. Tanaka." He waved goodbye with his rubber-gloved hand and disappeared into the gym to find new things to spritz.

"Why does Nick call him Annie?" I asked Levi, who joined me at the front desk.

"Trevor lost both his parents. His dad most recently. Nick must be mocking that."

When I turned to scowl at Nick, he had disappeared.

Suddenly, Levi released a gasp reserved for bad actors in terrible horror films and gestured wildly at a wall-mounted file organizer. "A script!"

I leaned forward. "That's paper. Pink paper."

"That means it's a *revised* script! That can be revised again. To include a part for me. I knew I smelled opportunity."

"That was lavender… or vanilla." My pullover was still damp.

"He's right." Ramona placed two plastic cards in front of us. "It's Barbara Lou's script for the aerobics shoot tomorrow."

Levi bounced his fists on the desk. "Put me in the show, Ricky. You said it yourself—I'm versatile. I can play any role. I killed as Sister Mary Amnesia in an all-male production of *Nunsense*."

I tugged my earlobe. "An all-male production?"

"*Nunsense A-men!*" Levi steepled his fingers and bowed his head.

"Actually, we need more background players," Ramona said. "Especially guys."

Levi patted his chest. "It'd be my honor to film a cameo."

"Background."

"Atmospheric background." Levi smiled at Ramona. "Tell me more about my character. Of course, there are no small parts, blah, blah, blah, but how many lines do I get?"

Ramona's head nodding became head shaking. "No lines. Just follow along with Nicky and Barbara Lou. In the background."

"So I'm playing a mute. Interesting." He tapped his chin and paced. "The backstory practically writes itself. I'm already picturing the traumatic event that stifled his speech."

"Uh, I guess that's all fine," Ramona drawled. "As long as you whoop and holler along with everyone."

"A whooping, hollering mute. Inspired." Levi pursed his lips as he parsed that logic. "What part will my good buddy Sho play?"

"No. No, thank you. Good buddy Sho is not playing—"

"He has a limited range," Levi stage-whispered. "Is there a walk-on part? Maybe a stuffy butler or a judgey judge? Something that'll highlight his scowl?" He pointed at me. "Like what he's doing now."

Ramona's clenched expression was like looking in a mirror. "I guess if he wanted to pretend to be a judge who liked aerobics…"

"Levi, I'm not taking part in any aerobics." I reminded myself of that aspirational indifference. "How much do you pay background players?" I asked Ramona.

"I'm union," Levi announced. "Unless you don't want me to be. Wink, wink."

"It's voluntary. Just a fun thing to do. A lot of the kids from the community college join us."

"But you need people for tomorrow," I said. "Specifically male."

"Well, yes…"

"Tell you what. Take another twenty percent off our monthly membership, and you've got two background players for tomorrow."

The tip of Ramona's tongue poked out, her gaze drifting to the Rodeo Room. "Ten percent, and you dress yourselves."

"Deal."

Levi directed a second groan-inducing gasp at me. "You're not camera ready." He tweaked my nose. "When was your last facial?"

Slapping his hand away, I replied, "Uh, never."

Levi *tsk*ed while he skipped—literally—toward the exit. "Back in the spotlight again."

"Recall that we came here to train for a triathlon. For *your* bucket list."

"No one was invested in that storyline, Tanaka-san. This is much better. I already have ideas for your character's backstory."

I grabbed the door handle, wishing it were a push bumper. "I don't need additional backstory. My actual backstory has scarred me enough."

Levi tossed his head and glanced at Ramona. "Actors."

THE BELL ABOVE THE DOOR of the Cherry Blossom Café announced my arrival.

Hoping for a cup of green tea, I sat in a red vinyl swivel chair at the L-shaped counter and willed Jenny to appear.

Our sibling telepathy must still be crackling, because Jenny pushed through the saloon-style doors that separated the dining room and the kitchen, holding a steaming mug and flashing an impish grin.

"I figured you'd be on your way." She set the mug in front of me and swiped back a few wiry hairs that had escaped her barrette's hold, then pulled a brown paper sack from under the counter. "Special delivery."

The sack crinkled when I dug my hand inside and pulled out a box. "Pore strips? Who gave me these?"

"Who else?"

I set the box down. "I just left Levi at the gym. How does he do this?"

Waving a finger, Jenny said, "Here's my theory: he's got tiny tween elves everywhere."

I dug deeper into the sack. "With Levi, the most absurd explanation is usually the correct one." I grabbed another package and squinted at the label. "A face hammock? Drug stores sell this junk?"

"Pretty sure all this is from Levi's collection." Jenny grabbed the face hammock. "Remember these? Ma had one. She'd order all kinds of Japanese beauty contraptions. I used to sneak into her bathroom and try everything."

I lined up the tubes of exfoliant solution, night cream, mud masks, and under-eye serums along the counter.

"Levi sure wants you buffed and polished." She slipped the face hammock under the counter, assuming I hadn't noticed.

"I need to be camera ready."

As she unscrewed the eye serum to dab some on, she asked, "Do I want to know why?"

I crumpled the sack and tossed it onto the chair beside me. "I bartered for a reduced gym membership."

Jenny smirked. "Are you part of some before-and-after marketing campaign?"

"Har, har." I snatched back the serum. "It's worse. Tomorrow, I'll be an extra in an aerobics video starring Barbara Lou Sinclair."

If Jenny opened her mouth any wider, her eyes would pop out. "Where can I preorder? Tell me now."

I used my shoe to swivel my chair from left to right. "I need something to wear. Something *casual.*"

Jenny pointed toward the second floor, where she lived and where I squatted. "That trunk in your closet? It's got some old clothes from Ojii-chan in it. He always dressed for comfort."

"You carry around our deceased grandfather's leisurewear?"

My sister openly rebelled against our family's heritage and traditions, yet she hoarded all things Tanaka.

"I could never bring myself to throw it out. Oba-chan said I might need it someday." Jenny smiled. "Guess she was right."

Absently running my fingers across the ribbed end of the mud mask tube, I asked, "Do you know Nick Batista? He's a trainer at the Lone Star."

Jenny grabbed a rag to wipe the countertop. "Hmm, I know the name, but he's not a regular. I don't overhear any gossip about him. That's strange, now that I think about it." She squinted at me. "Hard to keep secrets in this town."

I fidgeted with the tube of night cream. "Well, avoid him if you can. Please."

Nodding, she asked, "You have some kind of encounter with this guy?"

"More like a confrontation."

Jenny's shoulders perked, and she stopped wiping. She opened her mouth, hesitated, and resumed wiping. "We had a bit of a confrontation here this afternoon too. FYI, don't flavor your coffee with anise."

I shivered. "Black licorice?"

"I'll tell you about it later."

I stared down my militia of beauty products, strategizing my counterattack.

"Something's bothering you, Sho-chan."

"I'm fine."

"*Fine* is your passive-aggressive code for everything but."

I snorted. "You sound like Ma."

Jenny slapped the rag against the counter, startling me.

Until recently, I'd disconnected from Jenny over a series of choices I considered reckless. Quitting an elite East Coast culinary program to move to Texas was only the most recent and the one we'd sparred over early into my visit.

We'd struck a nonverbal truce to avoid additional land-mine conversations, but I'd been keeping a lot of secrets: being held at gunpoint in my ICU, suffering from crippling panic attacks, and developing a prescription drug addiction, to name a few.

"I'm just grumpy, dreading tomorrow." My answer was technically true. "Levi will be in his element and prone to more shenanigans than usual."

For a moment at the gym, I'd felt like myself again—in control. The thought of my strutting around in my grandfather's leisurewear made all that seem silly.

"Tell you what," Jenny said. "We're closing for a few hours before dinner. Go upstairs and change, and I'll take us up some munchies. We can apply mud masks and pore strips and avoid sensitive topics of conversation."

I grimaced. "I'm not putting this goop on. What's in it for me?"

"You just compared me to Ma. Your head still being attached to your shoulders is gift enough."

"Nope. Try again."

"Fine. Munchies, your life, warm sake…"

"Keep going."

"And… I'll let you rip off my pore strips."

I reached for the crumpled sack to repack my beauty stash. "Deal."

"Really? My torture seals it?"

After grabbing my tea and supplies, I headed upstairs. "What can I say? It's an offer I couldn't refuse."

Chapter 4

ZIPPING THROUGH THE TOWN SQUARE at seven thirty a.m. in a Hello Kitty helmet was one kind of self-humiliation, but my athletic wear for my aerobics debut put me in a special circle of hell.

Discovering the Tanaka family treasures with Jenny was fun, mainly after a few sake bombs. But my dearly departed grandfather left fewer options than Jenny had remembered. We pieced together what we could, but Jenny suggested I stand in the back and avoid open flames.

The ankle-length raincoat I'd wrapped myself in furled behind me as I steered the Segway into the gym's parking lot.

Levi waved me over from the sidewalk. He wore a bubble-gum-pink tank and lime-green short-shorts speckled with neon confetti. "How do I look?"

"Like a busted piñata." Stepping off my environmentally responsible death trap, I cinched the belt of my raincoat tighter.

"Aerobics is the Halloween of fitness." He surveyed me with a lopsided grin. "What's with the raincoat? More early morning flashing?"

Ignoring him, I hustled through the front door of the Lone Star.

Levi galloped beside me. "So, I got here early, hoping for a tête-à-tête with the director…"

Shhh, shhh.

"What's that sound?" he asked.

I bit my lip and slowed my pace. "Who is the director?"

Shhh, shhh.

"Vaughn Sinclair. He's Barbara Lou's brother. Written, directed, and produced every video she's ever done—"

Shhh, shhh.

Levi stopped and glared. "Did you just shush me?"

I pulled the raincoat tighter and shook my head.

"Where's that sound coming from? Kind of a *shhh, shhh* sound."

Wincing, I replied, "It's me, all right? I'm the *shhh, shhh.*" I loosened the belt on my overcoat and popped the first button. "Don't laugh. I'm going to show you what's underneath."

"This same thing happened to me on Hollywood Boulevard. And I did, indeed, laugh."

I muttered profanities while unfastening the last button. Pulling the flaps of the overcoat open, I turned my head away.

Levi stood silently. Finally, he said, "Oh. My. *Pow.*" He made an explosion sound.

"I look ridiculous, don't I?"

"I've never seen anything like it. What happened to your pizzazzy beige? Your jaunty puce?"

Frowning, I looked down at my shimmering turquoise-and-white tracksuit. "Guess I'm making up for that. All at one time. I feel like I should be power walking at the mall."

"It's… so shiny." Levi held out his hand to touch it but jerked it back like I was a hot stove. "Is that lamé?"

"I don't know what that is."

"It's the thespian's textile: bold and flashy, and it'll pull focus from the lead. It's brilliant, Tanaka-san." He tipped an imaginary hat. "It's an honor to be your best bud."

"Well, now I'm nauseated." I wrapped the coat back around me.

Levi hopped behind me to slip it off my shoulders. "You'll be amazing." He folded the coat over his forearm. "And with that costume, no one will even notice your flat-footed movements."

"My flat-foo—"

"Now, before we go into the studio, I must warn you."

"Wait. Let me grab the ibuprofen in my coat pocket."

"Studios are my second home. I'll be back in my element. When I'm in my element, I'm prone to dramatics."

I blinked. "And…?"

"I can get demanding, unpredictable, and self-absorbed. It's all part of my process. I just don't want to shock you."

I blinked again but that time to process that Levi's confession was for his assurance, not mine. His acting jobs had dried up after his show's cancellation, though I'd first encountered him doing impromptu miming on the town square. I suspected he was nervous about the video. "Can you handle this? Do you want to leave?"

"What do you mean?"

"I mean you're a background player in an aerobics video, yet you're channeling Norma Desmond."

Levi dismissed me with a hand wave. "You know I don't follow politics."

"Norma Desmond? *Sunset Boulevard*? 'All right, Mr. DeMille, I'm ready for my close-up'?"

Levi tweaked my nose. "Then you should've used those pore strips!" He swung around to open the door to the Rodeo Room. "Spiffy tracksuits don't hide everything."

"Good morning, gentlemen." Ramona did a double take to absorb our aerobics-wear splendor. "You two certainly dressed the part."

I grabbed my raincoat from Levi. "Is it too much? I'll cover myself with this."

Ramona laughed. "You look perfect. A throwback to the good old days."

Levi waved his hands down his outfit. "But I think *this* could use something more."

"You think it needs… more?" Ramona stepped back to inspect Levi's outfit. "Um, well, I suppose we could add a—"

"Excuse me!"

I turned toward where the voice had come from, and a camera lens almost smacked me in the face.

"Would you tell me who you're wearing?" the man behind the camera asked in a nasal voice.

I glanced down at my tracksuit and back at the camera. "Who I'm wearing? Uh… my grandfather?"

Ramona placed a hand on the camera operator's shoulder and whispered something in his ear. The operator, a college-age kid, rolled his eyes and skulked away.

"Our interns are shooting some B-roll. Sorry."

"B-roll?"

"Vaughn likes all his movies to look authentic, so he shoots some behind-the-scenes footage. No one ever sees most of it, but it makes Vaughn happy."

A bespectacled man with thinning hair and wearing a phone holster approached. "Romy, has Barbie arrived yet?" He held a crumpled piece of yellow paper.

Levi gasped. "The script! And it's yellow!"

The man looked at the paper and back at Ramona.

"Vaughn, hun, you remember Mayor Blue used to be an actor. A famous one." That triggered her head-bobbing tic.

"Do I?" Vaughn pushed up his glasses.

"Is yellow better than pink?" I asked Levi.

"It means there's been another revision. Maybe they wrote a part for me after I signed my contract."

"Your *contract* is ten percent off pressed juice and extra towels."

"What about the Zumba?"

"Let me know when Barbie arrives," Vaughn said to his wife. "Please. We need to start."

"I'm sure *everyone* will know when she arrives," Ramona said. "Now, Mayor Blue, I have the perfect accessories for you. Come with me."

They both exited the studio, and I tried to relax and take in all the activity. Though it was just a local fitness shoot, it was interesting to see how everything came together.

Trevor stood to one side, watching Nick film. Using a contraption that looked like linked rubber chains, Nick curled his bicep, talking and smiling to the camera as he flexed.

"Absorbing all this aerobics magic?" I asked Trevor, who jumped a little in surprise. "Are you a fan of Nick's?"

Trevor furrowed his brow and smiled. "Mr. Nick's super motivating. He got me obsessed with fitness."

"What's he using for that bicep curl?" I pointed at the stretchy chain.

"A resistance band. I think that one's a prototype Marisol developed." Trevor indicated a small and slender young woman who stood behind Vaughn. She appeared to be filming the exercise with her phone camera, her long brown ponytail bouncing as she worked.

"What's her job?" I asked.

"She works for Mr. Nick," Trevor said. "She's an influencer."

I bit my lip to suppress a laugh. "What does she influence?"

"The internet, I guess."

"Um, Trevor." I cleared my throat. "Mayor Blue told me about your parents."

Trevor whipped his head around, his face flushed with alarm.

"I just wanted to say… What Nick called you the other day… He's a jerk. I've experienced some trauma, too, and I'm here if you ever want to talk."

"And… cut," Vaughn said. "Great work, Nicky. Take five, and we'll shoot the lower-body segment."

Marisol removed a handheld fan from the purse slung over her shoulder. She held it in front of Nick, who tilted his head back to get the full effect of the mechanically produced wind.

"Thanks, Mr. Tanaka. But I try not to think about that stuff." Trevor grabbed a water bottle from the ground. "Oh, dish soap and super-hot water. That'll get the lavender-oil stains out of your clothes."

I nodded. "Do you dabble in aromatherapy?"

Trevor pursed his lips. "I don't know what *dabble* means." With a quick wave, he scrambled over to Nick, who held his hand out for the water. "Super job, Mr. Nick."

"Did that look okay?" Nick asked Marisol. "Am I shiny? These lights are hot today."

"Because you're lighting this joint on fire." With her free hand, Marisol pulled a fluffy-headed brush from her purse and dotted it on Nick's cheeks and forehead. "You looked fab and yummy and all the things."

Marisol's confidence made me uncomfortable and drawn to her at the same time.

"Um, Mr. Nick, have you thought about shooting the bicep curl from a side angle?" Trevor asked.

Marisol's ponytail whipped through the air when she turned. "The towel boy directs too? Grand."

"I know it's not my place," Trevor continued, "but a side angle would also show the flex in your elbow and shoulder."

"Don't you have some toilets to plunge?" Marisol asked.

Nick drank from the water bottle. "Hmm, I've done that angle before."

"Three years ago, Mr. Nick, and it was super helpful for me in mastering my form. It was in *Belles, Buckaroos, and Burpees.*"

"Is that some kind of fitness cult?" Marisol snorted.

Nick's jaw twitched. "It's the name of my first video."

The brush dropped from Marisol's hand. As she fumbled to retrieve it, the purse strap slipped off her shoulder. "I'm joking. I *knew* that."

"Thanks for the tip, Annie," Nick said to Trevor, ignoring Marisol. "I'll ask Vaughn for another take."

"Whatever." Marisol jammed the fan and brush into her purse. "Take advice from your stalker." She flicked her wrist in Trevor's direction. "Go find a hoodie in a dark alley somewhere."

I shook my head. *Poor Trevor.* Perhaps I wasn't as drawn to Marisol as I thought.

"Are you Sho?" came a woman's voice from behind me.

I noticed her arched thick black eyebrows first, then her peroxided—almost white—hair, which was cropped short around her head and chin like a cap. She could have been in her late forties, but obvious plastic surgery had frozen her face in mid-surprise.

"I'm Celeste Gravell." She shook my hand. "I do background

for the workouts, but I also teach the newbies our basic moves. Got time to work with me?"

I nodded. "My friend's just getting a costume upgrade."

"Oh, I'm not worried about Mayor Blue," she said. "I've seen *Tween of the Crime*. Pole dancers study his shimmy shake."

I blinked. "Levi certainly has an eclectic skill set."

Celeste led me to the other side of the studio, then spun around and started marching in place. "Barbie breaks her routines into four basic moves. Follow me."

I did as I was told.

Celeste beamed. "Now pump your arms as you step to the side."

When I copied her, she nodded with approval.

"Move your shoulders forward with each step. Pull your torso back."

I struggled to do what she was describing, and she smiled sympathetically at my lurching movements.

"Loosen up. Have some fun," she said. "You look like a stomping robot. Roll your shoulders back."

"Right. Okay, how's this?"

"You haven't done anything yet."

"Oh."

"Okay, okay. Let's try this again. Go back to marching. I want you to keep your core nice and tight." Celeste contracted her stomach. "But relax those arms and legs a bit. Shake 'em out. Have some fun."

"Fun? When is marching fun?"

"You're getting it. Now take a small step to your right, and return to the marching. Repeat with a side step to the left. Watch me."

I did just that then did the move.

"Nice, Sho. Now take two steps to the right. Repeat on the left side."

I followed her lead, tripping some as I moved but staying upright.

"Nice double side step, Sho. Ready for a challenge?"

"There's more?"

"There's always more. When you take that second step to the right, dig your left foot behind you."

"Uh…"

"It's called a Grapevine. Watch me first."

I did, then I tried.

"You got it. You got it. You look like one of the Temptations."

"Really? I feel more like a California Raisin."

Celeste laughed. "You just need some self-confidence."

"I'll remember that. Thanks. You're a great teacher."

"Oh Em Gee!" someone beside me exclaimed. "Where did you get your fresh threads?"

Marisol, the alleged influencer, rushed me and inspected my tracksuit with her long fingernails.

"It belonged to my Ojii-chan. My grandfather." My cheeks burned from the attention.

Celeste clicked her tongue and folded her arms. She was no fan of Marisol.

"Vintage. I like. I like," Marisol said. "So hot."

"You're not wearing that for the shoot, are you, Noodle Arms?" Nick inserted himself into the conversation.

"This is all I have. Ramona seemed okay with it."

"It's more than okay." Marisol circled me, scratching the synthetic fabric with her nails. "Except you're dressed like a star, and…"

"You're no star," Nick said.

"Back off, Nicky." Celeste patted him on the chest. "The camera hardly stays on the background for more than a second. Nothing will distract from your expensively capped chompers."

"That's what these teeth are paid to do," Nick said. "We each have a part to play. Just making sure Noodle Arms here knows his."

"Stop calling me—"

"Whatever." Nick threw up his hands. "Vaughn will just stick him in the back behind the coeds. Where the camera won't find him."

"You may be a rising star, Nicky, but you're not ruling this roost yet," Celeste said. "Let me get back to my teaching."

Nick shrugged and walked away.

I shut my eyes and mumbled, "'Grant me the serenity to accept the things I cannot change…'"

"'The courage to change the things I can, and the wisdom to know the difference.'" Celeste leaned closer. "Refreshing to hear the Serenity Prayer here. We need more of that."

"It's… a…" Stiffening my posture made my blood rush to my head faster. "I had a community health requirement in nursing school. Mostly, I attended parent-to-be classes, but I also observed a Narcotics Anonymous meeting. Once."

"Then you're familiar with our Twelve Traditions."

The Twelve Traditions of NA were plastered on every piece of literature that my insistent psychiatrist had given me. Of course I was familiar.

Wait. Did Celeste refer to them as our *Twelve Traditions?*

"'Anonymity is the spiritual foundation of all our Traditions,'" she said, quoting the final tradition. "You're among friends, Sho. In case you ever need one." She patted my shoulder. "Now, remember to smile whenever the camera's on. Even if you're not feeling it. Pained expressions don't motivate viewers to exercise with us."

Levi leaped through the door. He'd added a lime-green sweatband and matching wrist warmers. I wondered if the videos came with sunglasses. In his arms, he cradled a small dog that he was feeding bacon bites.

Celeste smiled. "Hello, sweet baby."

"Well, hello yourself," Levi said.

"She's talking to the dog." I casually inspected Levi, who somehow traveled everywhere with bacon.

"I see Miss Tallulah found you." Celeste stroked the dog's rough reddish-brown coat.

"We've seen each other around town," Levi replied. "But this is our first formal introduction." He shot me an excited grin. "Remember her, Tanaka-san?"

The flat-faced Brussels griffon blinked at me and yawned. We'd seen her around Bluebonnet Hills several times, usually right before Levi and I wandered into danger. "We thought she was a stray."

"Lulah is a nomad," Celeste said. "She showed up a few weeks ago and adopted me. Though she's not very people-friendly, she seems to adore the mayor."

The door into the Rodeo Room burst open, and everyone heard and felt the impact. A woman with bug eyes and helmet hair loomed in the doorway.

"Where's Vaughn?" she asked. "I need to strangle him."

"Don't make direct eye contact, boys," Celeste said. "Bow your head, step into the darkness, and make room for the queen."

Chapter 5

BARBARA LOU SINCLAIR, queen supreme, commanded the studio with a jut of her chin. Her round eyes bulged when she scanned the room. She looked like she'd been poured into her two-sizes-too-small orange bodysuit and matching tutu. When she charged toward her brother, a duffel bag slung over her shoulder, she resembled a middle-aged sprite clomping through the forest.

"What's wrong, Barbie?" Vaughn sounded more exasperated than concerned. "We need to get going if you want a rehearsal first."

"You know precisely what's wrong." Barbara Lou unzipped

the duffel and removed the white pages of her script, which she flung to the floor. "You've reduced me to a background player in my workout."

Vaughn's eyes followed the script pages. "Where did you get this? Those pages aren't part of the shooting script."

"Don't deflect!" Barbara Lou's eyes bulged. "You've got me doing all the modified versions of Nick's exercises. Like some decrepit old lady. And now we're playing with toys? What's this about resistance bands?"

"It's a merchandising opportunity, Barbie. And a chance to pull in some new fans." Vaughn released a heavy sigh. "But I cut out the group exercises with the band. Nick's doing them now. Solo." He scuffed a shoe over the script pages. "You should never have seen this version."

"Being saddled with the modified exercises is not a good look for me." Barbara Lou stepped back and waved her hands over her clothing. "Speaking of a good look, you've dressed me like the headliner for a UT football halftime show. Orange is *not* my color. It's *no one's* color."

"It's my color." Nick patted his tanned cheeks. "Complements my skin tone, don'tcha think?"

"Of course you're behind this." Barbara Lou leaned to the side to glare at Marisol. "Or your handler is." She turned back to her brother. "My fans expect a certain level of quality from a Barbara Lou Sinclair production. Nicky and I don't need matching outfits. We look like a mother-son real estate team." She lowered her voice and widened her eyes. "Or inmates at the state penitentiary."

"What's that supposed to mean?" Nick asked loudly. "You saying I belong in prison?"

"That wasn't the implication." Barbara Lou's mouth tightened. "Hush up."

Nick delivered a mocking laugh. "Sure thing, madam.

I certainly don't want to frighten everyone. You know, just another angry brown dude in an orange jumpsuit."

"This escalated rather quickly," I said to Levi. "You suppose this is normal behavior for these two?"

"Like I told you, the star demands everyone's full attention. Orange you glad you have me around?" Levi quipped.

I rolled my eyes.

"Enough! Please." Vaughn held up his hands. To his sister, he said, "You're prominently featured in this video. I promise. Nobody sticks Barbie in a corner, right?" He turned to Nick. "You've got the solo video with the resistance band, so be a team player for me now, champ." Vaughn stepped back and lowered his hands. "And there's no time for costume changes. The orange stays."

Levi slapped my arm. "Orange you glad we're standing in the back?"

For variety, I added a groan to my eye roll.

Vaughn clapped. "Let's move, people. Barbie, do you want a rehearsal?"

"I'm ready." Nick flashed his shark's teeth.

Barbara Lou shook the energy of the argument from her hands. "Give me a minute to freshen up before we shoot the opening."

Vaughn spun around and noticed an intern with a raised handheld camera. "Erase whatever you just shot." He held his hand over the camera's lens as he walked forward, forcing the intern to retreat in kind.

Celeste slotted herself between Levi and me. "What did I miss, boys?" She held a royal-blue sweatband that glittered under the lights.

"Nice bling." Levi gave a thumbs-up. "You trying to upstage me?"

"Naw. Let's join forces to pull focus from both those divas." With a chuckle, Celeste slipped on the sweatband.

I pointed at the sweatband's embroidered logo of a black bird with a two-toned orange bill. "Is that a toucan?"

"Part of Marisol's line of athletic wear." Celeste touched the sequins, making light refract into my eyes. "I love how the color makes my hair sparkle."

I smiled. "Won't Barbara Lou go bonkers if she sees you?"

"Golly, I never thought of that." Celeste pressed a palm to her cheek. "I sure hope so."

Barbara Lou's shrieks diverted our attention to the other side of the studio. That didn't take long.

"Get that camera out of my face!" She held one hand in front of the lens and tossed her duffel bag to the floor with the other, then adjusted her outfit as a mark of regaining her composure. "Vaughn, we're not paying these interns to creep around with their cameras."

"We're unpaid," the intern in question muttered.

"All right, everyone. Take your places." Vaughn had an amazing ability to ignore anything happening around him.

Nick, who'd been lingering around the set, cleared his throat. "I need some water before we begin."

Barbara Lou let out an exasperated laugh. "Here we go."

"Now?" Vaughn asked. "We just had a break. Here, drink some of this new energy drink." He pushed a plastic bottle of pink liquid at Nick. "Lemme snap a photo of you while you're at it. It's a potential sponsor. Easy money."

"The amount of sugar in that will break Nicky's fast." Marisol staggered forward and slapped the bottle from Vaughn's hand, almost spilling the water cup she was drinking from.

Vaughn glared at Marisol, opening his mouth to say something to her.

"Annie, go grab my water from the locker room."

Trevor bobbed his head in acknowledgment and turned to leave.

"And put some hustle into it, Annie." Nick stepped toward him. "Sheesh, did your parents die from boredom? Waiting for you is like—"

"Enough." I curled my hands into fists.

Several gasps pinged off the walls, followed by icy silence.

Nick turned around, sporting a smirk that demanded to be smacked right off his face. Where was an inflatable push bumper when you needed one?

"Thought I heard a chirpy chirp back here. That you, Nurse Nightingale?" He cracked his neck and swaggered toward me.

I squeezed my fists tighter to absorb my anger.

Nick increased his speed then stooped so he could look me directly in the eyes. I didn't flinch.

"You got something to say to me…" His hands slowly crept toward me to adjust the collar of my tracksuit. "Noodle Arms?"

"I said *enough*. Don't speak to people like that."

Nick continued tugging at my collar, the fabric rubbing against my neck. "Guess I need to brush up on my bedside manner." He chuckled and glanced around for others to validate his humor. "Annie knows I'm joking around. Don'tcha, Annie?"

My hands tingled, so I released the fists. Sweat dotted my brow, but the sweatband absorbed it. "You don't humiliate people like that. It's not motivating. It's demeaning."

The sensation from my wobbling knees made me paranoid that I was signaling fear instead of my body's natural response to the adrenaline pumping through me.

Levi gripped my shoulder. "He's not worth it, Tanaka-san."

Nick poked the inside of his cheek with his tongue and spun around. "I need a minute, Vaughn."

"Nicky, baby, we've got to shoot something. I only have this crew for a few more hours."

"Then you'd better wait. Or shoot around me." He scoffed. "Barbara Lou can certainly fill an entire frame."

"Pig," she spat in response.

"Take *her* with you." Vaughn waved his hand at Marisol.

Nick stalked back to grip Marisol by the arm and escorted her from the studio.

"What a jerk," I said.

"He's been under some stress," Celeste replied.

"Don't defend him," I said, perhaps too loudly. "Don't normalize that disgusting behavior."

Celeste raised her hands. "I meant he's usually not this agitated—"

"Maybe he needs another trip to church with you."

We all turned to Barbara Lou, who had Celeste in her sights.

Celeste smoothed her hair, an obvious attempt to highlight her sweatband. "Say that again, Barbie? I couldn't quite hear you." Her voice dripped with honey, but the underlying tone was thick with acid.

"You heard me." Barbara Lou approached. "Your faith-based rehabilitation ploy is failing. Looks like the old mare needs a new sugar bowl." She adjusted her tiara and retook her mark. "And take that sweatband off before I make Vaughn do it. Save the royal blue for the royals."

"Said the walking, talking orange juice carton," Celeste muttered.

Nick jogged back into the studio and ran circles around the set, pumping his fist in the air. "Vaughn, I'm ready."

"You sure, Nicky?"

"Let's get this done."

"Everyone, into position." Vaughn stepped into the darkness with the cameras and crew. "Let's shoot some film here."

"Uh, we're all digital," said an intern, who'd chosen the wrong moment to be literal.

Vaughn held up three fingers for a countdown. "And three, two…"

All the background players clapped, hollered, and bounced. Well, I didn't bounce. Barbara Lou and Nick jogged in from opposite corners and took center stage.

"Howdy!" Barbara Lou exclaimed with all her perkiness. "Y'all ready to lasso those pesky pounds and put 'em out to pasture?"

"Spend thirly minutes—" Nick slurred.

"Stop! Stop!" Vaughn called from the blackness.

"My bad, Vaughn. Got a little tongue-tied." Nick jogged back off the stage. "*Thirty* minutes, *thirty* minutes," he repeated quietly.

"Still rolling. Going again. And three, two…"

Clap. Holler. Bounce. Clap. Holler. Bounce.

"Howdy! Y'all ready to lasso those pesky pounds and put 'em out to pasture?" Barbara Lou threw an imaginary lasso at the camera and pantomimed dragging it in.

"Then we're gonna… Let's get some…" Nick grunted in frustration.

"Cut! Nicky, baby, what's the problem?"

"Sorry! I got lost for a second." Nick's tank top pulled up when he bent over, revealing a nicotine patch.

"That explains the sudden jolt of energy," I said.

"All right, everyone back to ones…"

"Where are you going?" Levi asked when I stepped forward.

"Are you fasting?" I asked Nick. "Fasting while wearing a nicotine patch can be dangerous."

Nick pressed his hand into my shoulder. "Keep your voice down. Patches don't break the fast. I Googled it." He stumbled, steadying himself with my shoulder.

"Google science aside, your blood sugar is dropping."

Nick closed his eyes and breathed deeply before growling into the darkness. "Annie, where's my water?"

"You need fruit juice or a soft drink." I reached for his hand, which he jerked away.

"What the…? We going steady now, Nurse Nancy?"

"I was trying to check your pulse." My insides twisted like a wrung-out dishrag, causing me to double over.

Trevor bounded into the light with the water bottle. Nick grabbed it with a grunt, flipped the lid, and knocked his head back to drink. Satisfied, he released a shuddering breath and pushed the bottle back to Trevor. "Ready. Let's go."

"You heard the man." Vaughn's voice came from somewhere in the darkness. "Let's knock this out in one take, all right?"

"He's not fine," I said to Levi, stumbling back in line. "He's going to pass out."

"Are *you* going to pass out, Tanaka-san? You're pale. And sweating. Maybe you should sit this one—"

I tried to stand straighter, inhaling through my nostrils. "I'll be fine. Mild nausea."

"Barbie, Nick, take your marks," Vaughn instructed. "Roll cameras. And three, two…"

Clap, holler, bounce. Clap, holler, bounce.

"Howdy! Y'all ready to lasso those pesky pounds and put 'em out to pasture?"

"Spend thirty minutes with me and Barbara New. Uh, Barley Blue…" Nick rocked back on his heels and swayed.

"Vaughn, stop. Stop!" Barbara Lou waved her hands.

Poorly veiled scowls and worried whispers erupted from those around us at the back. Levi looked at me with a furrowed brow. I tried to speak, but my mouth was so dry that my tongue just dragged across my lips. The heat from the overhead lights blazed down on my skin, which felt sunburned. When I glanced up, sparklers of light danced across my vision.

"Nicky, sweetheart," Barbara Lou said gently, "let's go lie down for a bit. We can do this later."

Nick held out his arm to silence her, then inhaled deeply and stood upright. "I'm okay now."

Then he dropped to the floor.

THE LAPELS OF MY TRACKSUIT felt like steel cords against my chest. I yanked at the zipper, desperate for relief, but it wouldn't budge.

"Tanaka-san."

As I darted my eyes back and forth, the room spun while the walls expanded and contracted around me. Lines of focus sharpened, while other lines blurred.

"Tanaka-san."

Cooler air blasted my chest, chilling the sweat that had formed on my back and neck. The zipper of my tracksuit was pulled halfway down. *How'd that happen?*

"Tanaka-san."

Levi's blue eyes and rocker's lips sharpened into focus. The room continued to spin, but Levi held his ground in the center of it all. A raspy sound pushed past my lips. "I'm… I'm having a…"

"A panic attack, I know. Don't speak. Just focus, okay? Let's try five-four-three-two-one."

I panted. "Counting?"

"That technique you taught me to control your breathing. Name five things you can see."

"Oh… right." I focused on Levi, attempting to wrestle with my intake. "One: you in that ridiculous outfit."

"I see you've still got that sparkling personality. Next."

"Number two. Uhhh…" My eyes drifted up and over Levi's shoulder. Trevor stood behind Levi, wearing rubber gloves and a respirator mask. "I see Trevor dressed as a radioactive bug from a 1950s B horror film."

Levi chuckled and glanced behind him. "He must have been cleaning toilets when the commotion happened."

Sounds rolled in and crashed against me—the panicked voices of the college coed extras and a high-pitched wail that sounded like it had come from Barbara Lou. My breath caught. "Nick."

"Don't think about that now." Levi clapped to regain my attention. "Number three."

"I need to check his pulse." I adjusted my weight to stand up, but gravity pushed me back down.

"Number three," Levi repeated.

"Pulse," I said. "CPR. Nick needs help."

"He's gone, Tanaka-san. There's nothing you can do."

"I should have… It's my job…"

"Focus. Number three."

I tilted my head and let my eyes continue to drift. "A water bottle… Nick's lifeless body…"

"Okay, let's stop there." Levi adjusted his crouch to conceal Nick. "What about four things you can touch?"

I inhaled through my nose and shut my eyes to concentrate. My breathing was starting to regulate. I pushed my palms into the floor and massaged my fingers to gain some sensation in my fingertips. "Number one, the floor." I moved my hand up a pant leg and made crinkle noises. "Two, Ojii-chan's tracksuit."

"Here, hun." Ramona thrust a cup of water at me.

I shook my head.

"You're in shock, hun. Drink this."

I swatted my hand toward the water, causing Ramona to jump back with a yelp. "I said no!" My head felt heavy and hazy, like I'd woken up with a hangover.

"Thanks, Ramona." Levi reached for the water. "I'll make sure he drinks it."

Focusing on my pant leg, I avoided Levi's stare. The shuffling to my left indicated Ramona had walked away.

"Hey," Levi whispered, leaning forward. "You're not… *on* something, are you?"

I picked at the turquoise fabric, trying to understand the question. "*On* something?"

"You're acting differently today. Good differently, but I mean, the colorful outfit, the confrontation with Nick. I just wondered if…"

I finally understood the question. "*On* something. Perhaps drugs?" Avoiding Levi's gaze, I flicked my fingers over the zipper, pulling it up and pushing it down. *What happened to me? When did wearing something different, having some fun, and standing up for someone else signal I was using drugs?* "I don't want any water. That's all."

"Okay."

I studied the water bottle on the ground. It had rolled away when Nick collapsed. Something didn't feel right.

I gasped. "The water." I rose to stand again but flopped back with little success. Pointing, I repeated, "The water."

Levi craned his head. "You're right, Tanaka-san." He stood and pointed at the bottle. "No one touch that water bottle," he commanded the room. "It could be evidence."

"Where are the…? Did you call…?" I heard myself ask, but my voice felt disconnected.

"I called Chief Malone," Levi said. "She's on her way."

"Who else drank the water?" I glared at the cup Ramona had brought me.

"Heavens, Marisol!" Celeste's voice rang out from somewhere to my right. "Where did she go? Did anyone see where Nick took her?" She ran into the center of the stage, swiveling in all directions, before disappearing into the main gym.

Trevor shuffled to Levi's side, having removed his gloves and mask. "Mayor Blue?"

"Hey, Trev, you okay, man?" Levi patted his shoulder.

Trevor swallowed, standing tall as if he was gathering the courage to speak.

"You killed him!" someone above me shouted in a shrill voice.

I looked up to see Barbara Lou in all her fiery orange rage. Claustrophobia was kicking in, causing me to push against the wall.

"Excuse me," Levi spat back at my accuser. "Nick spent most of the morning hurling insults at everyone here. Unless you think being compared to a parade float is a compliment."

Barbara Lou recoiled as if he'd slapped her. "He was doing just fine until your staff had to rile him up."

"I'm not his staff." *Oh, what's the point?* Harsh words flew around me like arrows. I pushed back into the wall and closed my eyes. "Nick didn't appear rattled by our conversation," I said finally. "Besides, it wasn't until he took a swig from that water bottle..."

My eyes popped open and landed on Trevor's shuffling feet. I inhaled sharply. "You gave Nick his water. His special filtered water. Right after he humiliated you in front of everyone."

Trevor ran a hand through his curly hair. "The police chief... She hates me."

"I'm sure." Levi smiled. "You got a criminal record for jay-walking to the malt shop?"

"No," Trevor said with a slight laugh. "But a few days ago, Mr. Nick, he called the cops on me."

"Nick? Why?"

"He... He caught me outside his house. Said I was stalking him."

"Stalking him?" Levi gave a dismissive laugh before concern tightened his eyes. "Were you?"

"I... I just wanted to talk, outside of work, you know? Get some advice. Mr. Nick got super angry. He said it couldn't keep doing this."

"This wasn't the first time Nick accused you of stalking?" I asked.

Police sirens wailed in the distance.

"It wasn't me, was it?" Trevor's voice rose in hysterics. "I brought him the wrong bottle, or someone slipped something into the pitcher. Nick filled it himself and set it in his locker. I just poured it."

Levi and I stared at each other for a moment. Though I sensed Trevor's desperation, I was too exhausted to think.

The sirens' blare grew closer and closer, and the murmurs around the room grew louder and louder until they had reached a ceaseless white noise.

"Everyone needs to chill." Levi raised his hands to his head. "Tanaka-san, stay there, and breathe. I'll go outside and meet Chief Malone. Trevor, cooperate with the police, but keep your answers brief. We don't know what happened here, so don't go incriminating yourself. Got it?"

Trevor nodded, but his vacant expression communicated he wasn't listening. He was lost in his thoughts rather than heeding Levi's surprisingly logical advice. I'd have told him that if I weren't busy trying not to pass out.

I shut my eyes, leaned back against the wall, and listened to the sirens.

Chapter 6

THE HUM OF THE CEILING FAN nudged me awake. It felt good to be back in my bedroom, on the second floor of the Cherry Blossom, even if I didn't remember how I'd gotten there from the Lone Star.

The entire Bluebonnet Hills emergency response team had arrived to assist Nick. The town of two thousand residents included three police officers, including Chief Malone, and emergency medical services. EMTs administered several rounds of CPR to Nick but to no avail. Nick was pronounced dead at the scene.

Barbara Lou's screaming hung heavily in my thoughts. *You killed him!*

Did I? Not directly, but when my medical training should have kicked in, I dissolved into sweat and dry heaves.

Confronting Nick had been out of character, but it bothered me that Levi thought drugs were driving the behavior. I couldn't decide what knotted my stomach more: the accusation or that, at that moment, drugs were all I wanted.

A soft knock came at my door, which Levi pushed open. With a flourish, he presented a nearly bare plate. *"Bon appétit."*

"This is a sprig of parsley."

"Mmm, keto."

"It's not keto! It was one of Jenny's breakfast sandwiches. Where's my smoked salmon and slightly runny egg pressed between fluffy Hokkaido milk bread?"

"Hard to remember." Levi picked something from his teeth. "It was so long ago."

I pushed away the covers and grabbed a pair of chinos. "It was thirty seconds ago. You walked fifteen steps from the café to here."

Trevor's throat clearing and feet shuffling drew my attention to the doorway.

"The police interviewed him again this morning," Levi said. "He needs our help."

I shook the wrinkles from the white polo in my suitcase and stepped behind the shoji screen to change. "Don't the police normally interview witnesses several times?"

"Witnesses and suspects," Levi said.

"The cops keep asking about my relationship with Nick. You know, before he died." My bed frame groaned when Trevor took a seat. "Chief Malone thinks I'm hiding something."

"Aren't you? Nick accused you of breaking into his home." I adjusted my collar and returned from behind the screen. Jenny

must have expected I'd have to dress in front of uninvited guests—
primarily Levi, who'd spun a chair around and straddled it.

"That situation has nothing to do with Nick dying," Trevor
said. "It's a super embarrassing misunderstanding. I can't lose
my job."

"You wash towels and mop sweat." I sat on the opposite corner
of the bed. "You'll find something more fulfilling."

"Mr. Nick started in my job, and look what happened to him."
Trevor cocked his head. "You know what I mean. Anyway, the
community college has this health program that also teaches
stuff like business and finance. I want a career in the industry,
and working at the Lone Star gives me some experience."

I nodded. "If you truly believe the police suspect you of something, start at the beginning. Did you break into Nick's house?"

"I was making a delivery."

"Delivering what?"

Trevor turned away. "Nick had a group exercise class that
night. I always made deliveries when he wasn't around. His
hazing got a little old."

"Did you have a key?"

"And another one for the gate." Trevor flopped backward
onto the bed like he was in a dorm room. "Nick told me to keep
quiet about the keys so that Barbara Lou wouldn't find out. It
was her house, after all."

As Levi scooted closer, the legs of his chair scraped the floor.
"Nick lived with Barbara Lou?"

"He lived in her guesthouse, but she's always working." Trev-
or's head swayed as he watched the rotating fan blades. "Except
the night I made my delivery. That's the embarrassing part of
the story. I caught Barbara Lou in the guesthouse. Trashing it."

"Trashing?"

"She'd emptied his drawers. Papers and stuff were all over
the floor. Then Nick came home early. His class had gotten

canceled." Trevor's shoe twitched as if the wind had blown it. "Ms. Barbara Lou, she got nervous, I guess. She told Nick she'd caught me sneaking around."

"With a set of house keys?" Levi slapped his knee. "I bet she flipped when you whipped those out."

Trevor's foot twitch increased to a jiggle. "Mr. Nick had made me promise not to say anything. I didn't want to get him in trouble or me to lose my job."

"This situation didn't convince you to break that promise?" I asked. Trevor's body language explained why he'd been reinterviewed by the police. His lack of eye contact and dancing feet revealed all his half truths. "I'll ask again: what were you delivering to Nick?"

"Considering how Nick treated you, why keep his secrets?" Levi asked.

Trevor sat up and sighed. "I was delivering his vape juice."

"His vape… Nick vaped?" That didn't fit with my perception of a trainer.

"Ms. Ramona confronted him about his smoking," Trevor said. "Gym members were complaining about the smell. They were canceling their training sessions or skipping Nick's classes. Vaping made Nick stop smelling like smoke, but the juice comes in all these crazy flavors."

"Nick couldn't buy his own vape juice?" Levi asked.

"He didn't want anyone in his business. And I was the one who told Ms. Ramona what the members were saying about Nick's smoking." Trevor's head slumped. "I didn't know it was a secret. I thought it was obvious. Ramona said she'd fire Nick if he didn't stop smoking."

Nick saw confrontation as a challenge. I'd had firsthand experience with that. He'd likely taken glee in circumventing Ramona's request and making Trevor his vape-juice runner. "That's why you had keys to his house. Nick didn't want anyone discovering his secret, particularly his fitness-costar-slash-landlady."

"I understand why all this would embarrass you," Levi said, "but it's not a motive for murder."

"We don't know he was murdered," I said. Nick was a red-meat eater with questionable dietary practices and addicted to nicotine. Didn't those better explain his death than murder? "Aside from your handing Nick the *possibly* poisoned water bottle, I doubt the police suspect you of any wrongdoing. They'll confirm your story. You have keys to the guesthouse, and the vape shop owner will recognize you. What did Chief Malone say when you shared all this?"

Trevor picked at the stitching on the bed quilt.

Sighing, I said, "This *dream job* of yours isn't worth all this."

"You don't understand." Trevor faced me, but I could barely hear him. "Yesterday, when you asked how I knew stuff about oils? My dad was in a car accident that gave him real bad pain." He stood and stretched his neck. "We tried everything to relieve it, even those oils."

Homeopathy intrigued me, but my approach to medicine was always evidence-based science. Admittedly, that concerned my parents and grandparents, who wanted me to embrace more Eastern, homeopathic philosophies.

"Nothing worked," Trevor continued, "but Dad didn't survive much longer…" He held his breath, a tactic I'd also used to keep my emotions from spilling out. "Moving here, landing this job, thinking about college… it all seemed like a sign. I can't lose another thing."

"I lost my dad, too, right after the network canceled my show." Levi swung his legs around the chair and stood. "I'd never felt more alone."

"Was he an actor too?" Trevor asked.

"An amazing physical comedian. He had this rubber face and elastic limbs. I could never do what he could."

Levi always brightened when he described his father.

"Dad had a condition called young-onset dementia," he continued. "He experienced the same mental decline as the dementia you're familiar with. It just happens in younger people."

Then his face dimmed—not much, but I'd seen it enough to notice.

"It's possible this form of dementia is hereditary," Levi said.

Diagnosing dementia was a long, complicated process. No single lab test, brain scan, or spinal tap could definitively detect it. Levi had witnessed the man he worshiped suffer through years of misdiagnoses and mockery, and he feared the same fate.

"Dad and I watched reruns of *Tween of the Crime*," Trevor said. "They came on in the afternoons, between his naps."

"I'm honored to be part of those memories."

"I'm surprised there's no *Tween of the Crime* revival." Trevor's eyes widened. "It'd be super cool to see you in action again."

Levi scratched his chin as if he'd never considered the prospect. "I'd star in it, naturally. Though I'm a smidge too old to portray an authentic tween."

I snorted. "A smidge?"

Levi pointed at me. "That expression is exactly how Professor Killjoy looked when I beat him in the figure-skate-off at the annual Tween Follies."

"The figure-skate-off?"

"That wasn't Professor Killjoy," Trevor said. "That was Major Wet Noodle."

Levi waved that away. "No, I'd remember—"

"After you won the skate-off, you said, 'Don't get saucy. This, too, shall pasta.' Season one, episode twelve, 'Impastas on Ice.'"

I slapped my forehead, which oddly shook another theory loose. "Trevor, who else knew Nick vaped?"

"I didn't tell anyone. But he took long breaks away from the gym to do it. People noticed." His mouth went slack. "Do you think someone poisoned the vape juice, Mr. Tanaka?"

"It's hard to keep secrets in a small town," I said, repeating what my sister had told me. "Did you discover why Barbara Lou was in the guesthouse that night, rifling through Nick's things? What was she looking for?"

Trevor shrugged. "I must have arrived before she found it."

I supposed vaping was off-brand enough to jeopardize Barbara Lou's aerobics enterprise. Was that a sufficient motive? "Was there always friction between her and Nick?"

"Kinda. Ms. Barbara Lou could also be pretty clingy. She was always asking Nick where he'd been or where he was going. She can be a bit much."

"Nick mentioned breaking up with his girlfriend. Was that Barbara Lou?"

"Uh… I mean, she'd take Nick lunch at the gym. She never brought me lunch. Maybe they were together, or she wanted them to be."

"Trevor, go downstairs and order breakfast." Still annoyed about my vanishing breakfast sandwich, I scowled at Levi. But it seemed something had distracted him. "I'll be down soon. We can discuss another visit to Chief Malone."

After Trevor closed the door behind him, Levi collapsed in the chair. "How could I confuse Professor Killjoy with Major Wet Noodle?"

"They sound like totally different characters," I lied. "How many episodes did you shoot? Ninety-something?"

"Ninety-seven. Plus the two-part musical Arbor Day special. Plus the unaired episode the censors still deny exists."

I blinked. "With a show that nuanced, you'll understandably confuse plot points."

"Not me. At least, I didn't used to. Is this how it starts? Am I losing my memory?"

I shook my head. "In less than two months, you've moved here, uncovered massive town fraud, and become mayor. Now Trevor's woes have you thinking about your father. It's a lot."

"It's not just that. I'm forgetting my words, too. That's another dementia symptom. What's it called? Diphtheria?"

"Dysnomia."

"See? I forgot the word for forgetting words! What if I forget an important word… like *rib*?"

"Then I'll be concerned." I chuckled to lighten the mood. "How can I help?"

"Let's help Trevor. If someone killed Nick"—Levi waved his finger between us—"*we* can bring the perp to justice."

I waved my finger right back. "*We* aren't investigators."

"Please." Levi blew a raspberry. "You've got medical knowledge up the wazoo. You just pointed out two ways someone could have poisoned Nick. And I've got five seasons of my well-honed tween-stincts to draw on."

"Do these alleged tween-stincts come with an investigative license or law enforcement authority?"

Butting into Nick's death seemed ghoulish. Detective stories romanticized amateur sleuths—those town librarians or local authors who interfered with murder investigations based solely on hunches.

Still, Nick's death had reengaged my intellectual curiosity. His nicotine addiction aside, Nick appeared physically and mentally healthy. Did he go into sudden cardiac arrest from undiagnosed cardiomyopathy? Or was it a ruptured brain aneurism? Or was it murder?

That desire to dig for a diagnosis excited me, but I'd already failed to provide Nick with the medical help he deserved. What made me think I could, or even should, investigate his death?

Because there were more questions than answers.

"Remember your renewed commitment to diet and exercise?" I asked Levi.

He groaned. "Vaguely."

"I'll go with you to the gym tomorrow to work out. If we conveniently run into Barbara Lou, well, I can't stop you from questioning her."

Levi's lips puckered. "Oh, that's clever. We *exercise* as a cover."

"Sure. On one condition. We go grocery shopping after. I want to show you how to shop the perimeter of the store."

"We need to find you a hobby. Or a girlfriend." Levi stood and rested his hand on the doorknob. "Thank you, Tanaka-san. Seriously."

Where I'd failed Nick, I might help Levi. Exercise would benefit both of us, and whatever investigating Levi did would be healthy cognitive activity.

Besides, I'd only committed to a workout.

What's the worst that can happen?

Chapter 7

Barbara Lou gripped two dumbbells, performing lunges. Levi waved his gym card under the scanner, his lips pushed into a pout. "So much for our covert ops. She's right there, practically waiting for us."

I surveyed the near-empty gym. Only a few members ran on the treadmills, their feet striking the soft rubber, their gazes fixed on some imaginary finish line. I supposed the death of a trainer put a damper on an athlete's fitness goals.

"Let's stretch out before warming up on the treadmill. We don't want to accost Barbara Lou and accuse her of murder."

Levi shrugged. "I accused people of murder all the time on *Tween of the Crime.* Usually before a commercial break."

"Sounds like stealth deduction work. How did all that indiscriminate accusing work out?"

"Eventually, I'd accuse the right person, beginning the act-three musical-chase sequence."

I closed my eyes, willing myself not to debate the realities of life versus TV land. "Unfortunately, we'll have to improvise to make up for the absence of chase music."

On cue, the universe gave me the middle finger and blasted rock music on the overhead speakers. Trevor stood behind the front desk, grappling with the stereo system's volume.

Levi cocked his head in amusement. "Think you can outrun Barbara Lou to this beat?"

"Perhaps we should consider the potential weapons." I nodded at the two dumbbells she was holding. "Or I'll duck behind you and use you as a human shield."

Levi strode toward Barbara Lou. Her face was red with exertion, but the color deepened when she noticed Levi.

"Mayor Blue," she said in cold acknowledgment. "Enjoy your workout." She turned and lunged away from us.

"You remember my good buddy, Sho Tanaka." Levi galloped beside Barbara Lou, his grin bright.

Barbara Lou blew out a breath when she stepped out of a lunge. "Of course. The unstable accountant with two left feet."

"I'm not an accountant." I bristled and walked along her other side.

"My mistake." Her bullfrog eyes widened. "Seeing you in person reminds me of how foolish I behaved the other day, accusing you."

Of murder. Accusing me of murder. "It was a tragic experience," I said instead. "Everyone responds differently to the emotion of the moment."

"Exactly. It was ridiculous to think any runt would intimidate Nick." She turned and lunged in another direction.

When I opened my mouth to reply, only a gurgling noise came out.

"I assume you're both hovering because you have questions about Nick," she said. "Well, I told the police everything I know. Which is nothing."

I finally found my tongue. "He lived with you."

Barbara Lou grunted and stiffened her upper body. "He was my renter." She released a burst of air when she pushed up. "And I drafted his rent directly from the paycheck I gave him every month. One sweet business arrangement. Have a good workout, gentlemen."

"I wanted to ask you about the script," Levi said.

Barbara Lou held her lunge, her cheeks puffed. "What script?"

"When you burst onto the set—very dramatic, by the way, superb entrance—you flicked the script at your brother." Levi flicked his wrist, recreating Barbara Lou's paper assault.

"It's just one of Vaughn's fussy little details. Drives me nuts. I don't need scripts for my videos. No one needs one, but Vaughn thinks he's Spielberg."

"Exactly. He does everything a professional director in a big-budget movie would," Levi said. "That's why I wondered why your script was on white paper instead of pink."

"I'm the star." She batted her eyelashes. "Guess I merit a special color."

"Maybe, but you print first drafts on white paper. It's an industry standard. Paper color changes with each revision: blue, pink, yellow, green..." Levi shrugged. "Standards can vary, but as you said, Vaughn thinks he's Spielberg. I'd expect him to execute every little detail. Meaning the star of the show had an older version of the script than everyone else. Including us lowly background players."

Barbara Lou dropped the dumbbells to the mat and turned to Levi, her face a mix of annoyance and impatience. "What's your point?"

"You were upset that Vaughn, that his script, had you doing the modified exercises. You were the supporting player in your video. Maybe the change truly caught you by surprise. Or maybe you knew the script had been revised. Several times."

"And I just wanted to make an entrance?" Barbara Lou snickered and adjusted the sweatband that supported her helmet hair.

"Or you wanted us to believe you were surprised." He cocked his head to one side. "Are you that good an actress?"

Levi had used his knowledge to perfectly bait Barbara Lou.

She stepped toward Levi then maneuvered around him to grab a medicine ball on the rack behind him. She plopped down on the mat and motioned for us to follow. The three of us formed a triangle, and she pushed the medicine ball out from her chest. "I didn't kill Nick."

Levi caught the ball. "Neither did Trevor. We want to help him." He tossed the ball to me.

My fingers slipped, but I threw it back to Barbara Lou. "How did you get your script?"

"It came to the house, pushed through the mail slot, in an unmarked envelope."

"Is that how you usually get your scripts?" I asked.

She winced as she shot the ball at Levi. "I told you. Those scripts are Vaughn's thing. I used to choreograph all my routines, but Vaughn's worked with me since the beginning. He eventually learned my moves so well that he just writes them for me. The only thing I remember is that it reeked of perfume."

"What did it smell like?" Levi's nose was always ready for a challenge.

"Cheap. Which means it could've belonged to anyone. At the time, I assumed it was Ramona. She soaks herself in rose water."

With all the various smells assaulting my nostrils at the Lone Star, I had missed Ramona's perfume. "You think someone else delivered the script? Why?"

"After what happened to Nicky, I wonder if maybe someone was trying to get a rise out of me. Ramona, Celeste, that terrible Marisol."

"Not a fan of Marisol?" I asked.

"You witnessed her behavior at the shoot. Do you think she was high on life?" She threw the medicine ball at my face.

I caught it, but it bonked my nose and slipped slightly from my sweaty fingers. *Why is she asking me that question?* I scraped my fingertips against the rubber, tossed the ball to Levi, and asked, "What about Celeste?"

"She had the hots for Nicky. Even started taking him to church, as if that would seduce him. And the Methodist church, at that. Why take communion with grape juice when we Baptists use red wine? Snaring men is Celeste's hobby. She's certainly had enough husbands, mostly younger than she is. She's a real… what's the word? Mountain lion."

"Cougar." Levi tossed her the medicine ball.

"Whatever. Nicky rejected her. She's lost her appeal, especially after those plastic surgeries. Men want a real woman, not a human pincushion." She thrust the medicine ball back at my face. "So now she's jilted and mangled. That'd make me want to kill." Yipping with gleeful satisfaction at her dig, Barbara Lou popped up and bounded up the steps of the eight-foot stair-climber.

Levi and I stumbled after Barbara Lou and took the stair-climbers on either side of her.

She pushed several buttons and began to climb, surveying the gym like a royal would her subjects. "The only thing I've gained from Nick's death is an increased heart rate. At least I can shed a few extra pounds."

"You retake the spotlight." I fumbled with the machine's buttons, my feet wobbling on the steps. "No more costar."

Barbara Lou gripped the handrails. "The only thing I crave lately is mint chocolate chip ice cream. Double scoop and on a cone." Her voice became breathier as she climbed. "I've deprived myself of so many comforts to build this business. Now, at my age, I have to exercise twice as much to get half the results." She stabbed the plus sign on the stair-climber to increase its speed. "Nick was popular. With the ladies, for obvious reasons, but even men joined our workouts because of him. He appealed to a market segment I never could."

I pressed the minus sign on my stair-climber, as my calves were already burning. "You saw Nick as your successor?"

"Maybe, after I'd smoothed some of the rougher edges. Nick clawed his way out of some pretty dark holes and let fitness fuel his recovery. I admired that." She laughed. "I don't do this for the spotlight. I do it for all the ladies who've supported me. So I won't abandon them until I know there's someone else who can rally them. Celeste blew her chance." Her gaze drifted down into the gym, and she sighed wistfully. "But Nicky, he had something special behind all those muscles and teeth." Her eyes watered. "I'll miss him."

I sensed she was about to burst into tears. Instead, she wetted her lips. "I tell ya, if I were twenty years younger…"

I followed her bug eyes, which were leering at Trevor. He had his back to us, bent over, cleaning equipment.

Ramona said in singsong from below us, "Time to nourish the body, Barbie." She hefted a tumbler like it was the elixir of life. "I've been watching you ping-pong around this gym all morning. I can always tell when something's bothering you."

Barbara Lou turned off her machine and shot Ramona a withering look. "My dear, if you only knew what was bothering me."

"What is that?" I gazed into the tumbler of spring-green

sludge, and my watery eyes confirmed Ramona's fondness for rose water.

"Green tea smoothie. Blended with love."

Barbara Lou stepped down from the machine and grabbed the tumbler. She held her lips just above the straw and asked, "Did you slip anything else in here? Besides your *love*?"

Ramona stepped back in retreat. "It's just a smoothie, Barbie. I swear."

Barbara Lou kept her lips hovered over the straw as if taunting Ramona. Finally, she took a sip. "Yummy yum yum," she said, her tone thick with sarcasm.

Ramona's face went white, and she practically ran back behind the front desk.

Levi and I exchanged confused looks. History simmered behind the smoothie subtext.

Barbara Lou watched her sister-in-law retreat, sucking the rest of her green tea.

Chapter 8

"OBVIOUSLY, SHE WAS LYING," Levi said between bites.

We were eating lunch at the Cherry Blossom Café, which meant Levi was probably on his third or fourth meal of the day. I'd forced him onto the treadmill for half an hour, so he could replace all the toxins he'd sweated out with new ones.

We sat in our usual chairs along the lunch counter. Jenny had served us wagyu beef burgers with a side of crunchy Asian slaw.

"Really? Barbara Lou seemed brutally honest to me. What was she lying about?"

From the other side of the counter, Jenny shushed me. "He's eating."

"We'll be waiting all day then."

Levi turned to me. "I don't know the exact lie. That's part of the mystery."

"You know she was lying, but you don't know about what?" I sipped my green tea.

Setting down his burger, Levi said, "Barbara Lou is a suspect. Suspects always tell at least one lie and one truth, especially this early in the episode. It's a classic trope."

"I see. How long does this lie-truth pattern last?"

"Until the episode is over, obviously."

"Obviously. What about those of us who don't live in a TV show?"

"I can't talk to you when you're irrational." Levi shoveled a forkful of slaw into his mouth.

Odessa Schubert, the editor of the *Bluebonnet Bee*, roosted a few chairs down the counter, beside her identical twin sister, Abilene. "My sources say you're the prime suspect, too, Sho." She flipped the cover of a pocket-sized notebook. "Care to give me a quote?"

"Not a printable one. Prime suspect? You must be joking."

"Only a little." Odessa's smoker's growl sounded extra agitated. "I heard you pinned Nick to the ground and poured poisoned water down his throat."

I plonked my mug on the counter, hot tea sloshing over my thumb. "That's ridiculous! Where did you hear that?"

"A reporter never reveals her sources." Odessa pushed her coffee cup toward my sister. "Jenny, hon, I'm sorry, but this coffee's just awful today."

Jenny's face drooped. "Sorry, Miss Odessa. I'm trying something new. I'll get you a fresh cup."

"Well, I love it." Abilene waved a french fry in the air. "Cinnamon gives you such a warm, comfy-cozy feeling." Then she pointed her fry at me. "And don't listen to Odessa, dear. She's full of fake news. I heard you put Nick in a headlock and hog-tied him with your paw-paw's pants legs."

I choked on my tea and grabbed a napkin. "That scenario lacks all plausibility. I'd have had to take off my pants to do all that."

Abilene held her hands up in surrender. "I don't judge."

"None of that happened." I gritted my teeth and looked at Levi, who unsuccessfully suppressed his smile. "Levi was there. He'll corroborate my story."

"You know how unreliable eyewitness testimony is," he quipped. "Who knows what actually happened?"

"You do!"

Abilene sipped her coffee. "Any loss of life is tragic. But you don't need to be part of the town phone tree to know Nick was cruel and not much liked."

"Serves Barbara Lou right, if you ask me." Odessa folded her arms. "Tossing her friends aside for him."

Jenny returned with fresh coffee. "That's right. You ladies are good friends with Barbara Lou."

"Acquaintances." Odessa nodded her thanks for the coffee.

"We're not as close as we used to be," Abilene said. "We still square dance together, but that's about it."

"Traded in for newer models." Odessa ripped open three sugar packets. "You know, Abilene and I were in a lot of Barbara Lou's aerobics videos."

Levi dropped his burger and grabbed his phone, clearly intending to scour the internet for photographic evidence of the revelation.

"I loved *Cowgirls and Crunches*," Abilene said. "I wore a spotted cow leotard with fringe."

"Barbara Lou taught aerobics in our church basement. That's how she started. She wanted actual women in her videos, not a gaggle of fake-tanned, sun-kissed twigs."

"Sister!"

"It's true. She made us everyday gals believe we could be who we were and stay healthy. Until she didn't."

"Nick started doing the videos," Abilene continued. "And Odessa and I were told we didn't reflect the 'Barbara Lou Sinclair brand.'" She made air quotes before swatting the air in disgust. "Whatever that means."

"Means we were too old, Sister. They wanted less mutton and more lamb."

Abilene tutted. "But with Barbara Lou strutting beside Nick, surrounded by all those pretty young things from the community college, well, now *she* doesn't reflect her brand."

"You reap what you sow." Odessa waved a forkful of watermelon from her fruit cup.

"Sister! She tried to make it up to us."

Odessa let her fork clank onto her plate. "Please. She gave us a three-month gym membership and a personal training session with her man candy. After what she did to us, I'd never step foot in that gym."

"I did." Abilene shrugged. "Even tried the session with Nick. Wasn't for me."

"He could be… intense," I said, trying not to slander a dead man.

"Intense doesn't bother me." Abilene's eyes darted to her twin. "But he reeked of cigarette smoke." Her nose crinkled at the memory. "I'm terribly sensitive, and, well, I just don't think that's the best image for a trainer."

Trevor had mentioned that too. A smoking habit and a hearty diet of red meat could impact the health of even someone like Nick. Perhaps his heart was what had finally given out. "Who told you this?" I asked the Schubert sisters. "That you no longer represented Barbara Lou's brand?"

"Officially, it was Vaughn," Odessa said. "But you'd have to dig deep to find a spine on that doofus. It must have come from Barbara Lou."

Abilene pulled a tube of lipstick from her purse. "My money's on Ramona."

"Why's that?" Levi asked as he chewed.

Abilene spoke as she reapplied her lipstick. "She's the one with all the money now. All that land they purchased behind your old construction site to build the new gym? Ramona's family owns all of it."

I turned to Levi. "Did you know that?"

"It came up at a town council meeting, but I hadn't connected it to recent events." He dabbed the burger juices on his chin with a napkin.

I leaned forward and lowered my voice. "But do you think Barbara Lou is… is capable of murder?"

"Why not?" Odessa asked. "She dumped all of us for Nick. He had a hold on her." She snapped her fingers. "Love can quickly turn to hate."

Abilene sighed. "It's easier to see Barbara Lou as the killer than poor Trevor. I'm grateful you boys are helping him. He's no killer. He's our bingo caller."

That settled that.

"What Abilene means is Trevor volunteers a lot at the senior center. He's a good egg." Odessa bowed her head. "Y'all probably heard about our aunt Honey. She died a few weeks ago."

"Pancreatic cancer," Abilene said quietly.

"Trevor volunteers at the assisted living facility connected to the senior center. During her last week on this earth, he visited Honey in the hospice every day. He read to her, listened to music…"

"He brought her a vanilla bean cupcake." Abilene sniffed. "Her favorite."

"Like I said—" Odessa turned away when her voice broke. "He's a good egg."

After a moment of silence for Aunt Honey, I said, "I'm missing Barbara Lou's motive for murder. She admitted how exhausted she was, about wanting someone to take over." I turned to Levi. "If that was her truth, what was her lie? That Nick was the best person to continue that legacy?"

As Jenny removed the sisters' empty lunch plates, she said, "Women like Barbara Lou don't just hand over their empire."

"What do you mean?"

"She's an entrepreneur. I mean, she's unmarried, has no kids, and that business is her life. Barbara Lou worked decades to establish herself. She couldn't just flash a smile to build what she did. Nick made good window dressing, and Barbara Lou used that to grow her fan base. She's no dummy, but maybe Nick got too cocky, too demanding." Jenny set the plates in a nearby caddy. "I'd be pretty annoyed if some slab of meat with a fake tan and whitened teeth tried to push me out of the business I built. There's your motive."

Another silence fell over the lunch counter as everyone considered that. Levi raised his half-eaten burger in salute, causing Jenny to grin. My sister was a far more compatible partner in crime than I was.

The bell above the café's door jingled, announcing a customer.

"Afternoon, Chief." Odessa straightened in her chair at the sight of Chief Monday Malone. "Care to give the *Bee* a quote about the Nick Batista investigation?" Odessa clicked her pen and held it at the ready.

"Sure thing, Miz Schubert." Monday puckered her lips in concentration. "How 'bout 'Mr. Batista's cause of death is currently being investigated, but foul play has not been ruled out.'"

Odessa dropped her pen. "That's the same clichéd statement Officer Perkins gave me. Passive voice and all."

Monday raised her shoulders in an exaggerated shrug. "When there's more to say, I'll be sure to say it."

Growling something unintelligible, Odessa grabbed her purse. "Back to work. See you later, Sister."

Abilene removed a piece of paper from her purse and stood. "C'mon, Mr. Mayor. We've got work to do."

"What're y'all working on?" Monday asked.

"I'm helping Mayor Blue fix all the inaccuracies on his *Tween of the Crime* fan wiki." Abilene waved the paper. "It's my civic duty to right these injustices. Did you know there's no wiki entry for the 'lost' episode? The one censors deny the existence of?"

Monday's face locked in an amazingly neutral expression.

"Oh, and, Chief?" Abilene patted her hand. "If you arrest somebody for Nick's murder, could you wait until tomorrow? It's bingo night, and we need our caller. I'm down fifty dollars."

Monday blinked while Levi grabbed his half-eaten lunch and moved to a corner booth with Abilene.

"Bingo and wikis. Is that our local government in action?" Monday took a seat next to me.

"I don't know about bingo, but the wiki is one of Levi's side projects." I chuckled and stared through the serving window into the kitchen. Was this wiki work a manifestation of Levi's anxiety over inheriting his father's dementia? "He wants to leave a legacy behind. That's all."

"The man's barely thirty. Why does he need a legacy?" Monday fidgeted with a plastic menu. "He needs to be doing his job. I'm understaffed and underequipped. And that was before a murder investigation punched me in the gut."

"Murder?" I set down my mug. "You've confirmed that? Nick didn't die of a heart attack?"

Monday tapped the edge of the menu against the countertop. "For now, I'll just say his death looks mighty suspicious and leave it there. Okay?" She caught Jenny's attention and pointed at my mug. "I'll have one of those too."

"It's green tea," I said.

Monday gritted her teeth. "I'm a big tea drinker."

"You are?" Jenny asked.

Monday raised an eyebrow. "Is this some kinda news story? Do we need to get Miz Schubert back here for a quote?"

Jenny gasped. "This is about the cinnamon in the coffee, isn't it? How did you hear about it? Is it already on social?"

Monday waved her hands. "I don't know what you're talking about. I just wanted some tea."

"What's this coffee thing about anyway, sis?"

Jenny gestured behind us to a wooden box labeled *Suggestions*. "I'm harnessing the power of yes."

"The power of what-now?" Monday asked.

Jenny slouched. "It's for my marketing class. I draw a new suggestion every day and implement it. No matter what. My professor says the best results come from the most unexpected practices."

I stared into my mug. "You won't harness my tea, will you?"

"So far, just the coffee. I added anise yesterday."

Monday shivered. "I hate black licorice."

"It was Miss Odessa's suggestion. Supposed to help with digestion," Jenny said. "Miss Abilene hated it, too, so she countered with the cinnamon. I need more suggestions, or I'll end up refereeing their sibling rivalry."

I draped my arms around my mug, shielding it further. "How long will you be… harnessing your yes?"

"A week. Seven days of yes." Her smile brightened, and her shoulders perked back up. "You two should try it. It's all about mindset. Saying yes to everything opens up opportunities—"

"No," Monday and I said in tandem.

Jenny waved a hand in exasperation. "I'll go make your tea."

Monday rapped her fingers on the counter. "I swear, some mornings, I wake up and think I've landed in the Twilight Zone." She swiveled her chair toward me. "And you didn't come down to the station yesterday as I asked. So here I am, coming to you."

"Sorry. I've been distracted."

Monday surveyed me with her forest-green eyes. "Get a good workout this morning, Tanaka? Or were you and the mayor engaged in some tween-boy detecting?"

I burned the top of my lip with the tea. "We had an impromptu conversation with Barbara Lou. Nothing came of it."

"Uh-huh. Is this where I lecture y'all about interfering with an active police investigation?"

I shook my head. "Levi wanted some mental stimulation. It's harmless. When he gets this way, I white-knuckle my way through it."

"Hmm." She swiveled back to the counter and studied the menu. "Did Miz Sinclair say anything of interest?"

I shrugged. "She discussed her relationship with Nick."

"Romantic?"

"She described it as professional. Celeste wanted the romance. Took Nick to church with her a lot."

Jenny placed a mug in front of Monday before bustling off to serve other customers. Monday took a sip, and her face contorted from its bitter punch.

"It's been a while, but I sure don't remember church being a popular dating activity," she said.

"Barbara Lou would agree. Methodists serve grape juice instead of red wine."

"Methodist? We found a St. Benito chain on Nick." Monday plinked her nails against the mug. "What's your take on all this, Tanaka?"

I set down my mug. "Am I a suspect?"

"You wanna be?" She squinted at me before smiling. "I'd

like your opinion. You're a nurse. You've seen strange things on the job."

"Your toxicology report isn't back yet, eh?"

Monday gently pounded her fist on the counter. "My leads are drying up faster than a West Texas dust storm."

"Have you contacted the Texas Rangers? Asked them for help?"

"I don't need the Rangers. I can manage my own investigation."

"Sorry. I didn't mean to imply—"

"What's your story, Tanaka?" She pushed the mug away. "You seem like a decent guy. What are you doing in Bluebonnet Hills? Besides playing Nanny Poppycock Two-Point-Oh?"

"I was helping Jenny with the café's finances, but she seems to—Nanny Who-dee Who?"

"Poppycock. Levi's sidekick in *Tween of the Crime*. One of 'em anyway."

I grinned and said in a singsong, "You watched *Tween of the Crime*."

Monday shushed me and turned around to check for eavesdroppers. "I might have seen a few episodes. Years ago."

"Did you hang posters of Levi on your bedroom ceiling too?"

Monday's face reddened, but her lips curled into a tight smile. "There might have been a poster or two. Got 'em from those magazines. Levi always had staple holes in his face." She glanced behind her again and chuckled. "Funny. When I see him now, I still see all those holes and think about who put 'em there." She knocked on the counter and stood. "Stay out of trouble, Tanaka. Thanks for the tea."

IN THE GROCERY STORE, Levi raised a bundle of bok choy to his nose and inhaled. "This demented lettuce smells like wet leaves."

"It's like cabbage but with a nutty aftertaste and is packed with antioxidants," I replied.

"Yay. Nothing screams comfort food like boiled cabbage."

"It's great in stir fries too. I'm sure Jenny's cooked you something with it." I took the bok choy from Levi and stuck it into a shopping bag. "Let's move on to peppers. I want to teach you the significance of their color. Did you know a single red bell pepper contains over two hundred percent of your daily vitamin C intake?"

Levi's head drooped sideways. "No one should know that, Tanaka-san."

As I pushed the cart to the vegetable cooler, I continued. "I have a quick, easy recipe for Mediterranean peppers stuffed with artichoke hearts, cherry tomatoes, feta cheese, and couscous. You won't miss the meat."

"Speaking of couscous, you need a new name."

I'd gotten used to Levi's non sequiturs. "Toss me two peppers. Red." I caught the peppers, popped them into the bag, and pushed the cart along. "What's wrong with my name?"

"Sho Tanaka? Sounds made-up, like a character for a movie or a TV show."

"How about for a book?"

"You know my feelings about reading." Levi tapped his boot against the floor. "You need something zippy, like Dr. Watson or Captain Hastings. Every detective's sidekick needs a cool name."

I stopped. "You think I'm *your* sidekick?"

"Obviously. On *Tween of the Crime*, I had my nannies. My favorite was Nanny Poppycock—soft and cuddly on the inside but firm and crusty on the outside. Just like her baked-from-scratch scones." Levi scratched his chin with a bunch of asparagus. "You're pretty crusty, but we can't call you Nanny Poppycock."

"Darn. That's the name I wanted. Oh well, Sho Tanaka will have to do. It's been good enough for the last thirty-something years. Besides, I don't like being referred to as a *sidekick*. Sidekicks can be impulsive or bumbling."

Levi continued using the asparagus to scratch his chin. It wasn't on the list, but we would have to buy it. His eyes brightened with inspiration. "How about deputy?"

"Deputy?"

"Yeah, we're in Texas. I need a take-charge, no-nonsense deputy." He snapped his fingers. "Plus, deputies get a much flashier wardrobe than regular sidekicks."

I pried the asparagus away and placed it in the cart. "I suppose deputy could work." Then I kicked my shoe into the wheel of the cart, realizing I'd once again engaged in Levi's ridiculousness.

"Ooh, look!" Levi gestured toward the bakery.

The glass cases were loaded with fresh bread, pies, and cakes. The scents of dough mixed with butter were intoxicating to those who craved flaky, tooth-rotting cholesterol and artery plaque.

"Too many carbs, but I have a substitute for you," I said. "A real treat. Coconut. Flour. Tortillas."

Levi sighed. "Stick a pin in that fun bomb. I meant, 'Ooh, look, there's Vaughn and Ramona.' Let's go over there and question them."

"Perfect. That strategy worked so well with Barbara Lou." I faced the cooler stacked with plastic containers of berries. "Berries will curb your sweet tooth," I said. "Blueberries and raspberries are both packed with antioxidants. And you can freeze leftovers for smoo—"

A crash sounded behind me. I looked over my shoulder, locking my eyes on Levi, who had rammed our cart into Vaughn's. The French bread Vaughn had just picked up lay crushed under his wheel next to his dropped phone.

"Oh, I'm so sorry. The cart just got away from me." Levi swiped his hands down his jeans dramatically. "My hands are so slimy from bok choy."

I rolled my eyes and grabbed a container of raspberries.

"No harm." Vaughn bent over to pick up his phone and the crushed bread. An online poker game showed on the screen. "You two certainly spend a lot of time together."

I placed the raspberries in the cart. "I'm helping Levi eat healthier by only shopping the perimeter of the store."

Vaughn focused on his game. "I suppose your accounting career leaves little time for hobbies."

"I'm not an accountant." *Again, probably not what I should clarify.*

"Such a coincidence we ran into you boys," Ramona said. "I just spoke to your sister about our nifty surprise."

"My sister?" I asked, bracing myself.

"We're finishing the aerobics video tomorrow," she said, "and we want you both in it!"

"Without Nick?" I asked.

"No fear. I've been a dutiful understudy," Levi said.

"The police haven't allowed us back in the Rodeo Room, so we'll be in our smaller studio." Ramona's plastic smile appeared. "It'll be more intimate and appropriate now that Barbara Lou will do the video without a costar."

To his credit, Levi remained composed and assaulted no one with the bok choy.

Ramona continued, "Jenny was overjoyed when I told her the news. Even offered to wash and press your tracksuit."

"I can't wait to thank her." I would have to ignore any payback for my overzealous pore-strip ripping.

"The deputy and I will be there," Levi said. "It's been a long time since I was on such a professionally run set. Well, besides the death and all that."

Vaughn placed a fresh loaf of bread in his cart, looking as though he wished he were doing anything but talking to us. "Thank you for saying that."

"In fact," Levi continued, "I was just telling Tanaka-san I bet you do everything to industry standard. For example, I noticed you printed your script on yellow paper. Does that mean those pages were for the fourth draft?"

Vaughn blushed. "I appreciate your noticing those details, Mayor Blue. I get a lot of ribbing about stuff like that from my wife and sister."

Ramona slapped his shoulder. "Oh, you jokester." She turned to us. "Isn't he a jokester?"

He wasn't tickling my funny bone, but comedy was subjective.

"But your sister's script, the one having her do all the modified exercises, was printed on white paper. How did she get that version?"

"I… I couldn't say. I don't even remember printing it. Drafting that version was about catharsis. I'd just learned that—"

Ramona yanked her husband's shirtsleeve, causing him to stop talking. Vaughn's mouth clamped shut, his cheeks puffing.

"Just learned what?" I asked.

Vaughn exhaled, swallowed, and said, "Nothing. Anyway, it was a mistake. Never meant for anyone to see it. Barbie and I've talked since, and she understands now."

"Why would someone want Barbara Lou to see that original script?"

Vaughn pushed his glasses up. "I had the correct script waiting for her at the gym. She never picked it up, which is not unlike Barbara Lou."

I recalled the pink pages of the script we'd seen that first day at the Lone Star. Someone wanted Barbara Lou to see those pages. But who and why? Could Nick have slipped them to her, perhaps delivering them to Barbara Lou's house during one of his extended smoke breaks? That raised some other questions for me.

"How long has Nick worked for you? No one in town appears

to know much about him before he arrived in Bluebonnet Hills. Like he appeared one day."

Ramona laughed as if that was a ridiculous statement. Vaughn, however, adjusted his glasses again and said, "I suppose he did. Appear one day, that is. He showed up at the Lone Star, looking for work. Barbara Lou took an instant liking to him, which was odd. Nick looked very different back then—"

"But he always had charisma," Ramona interrupted. "And he was a hard worker. We were in our old location, so it needed a lot more care and attention. Nicky pitched in wherever, folding towels or taking out the trash."

"He went from that to starring in aerobics videos?" I asked, puzzled.

"As Romy said, Nick always had charisma. My camera loved him almost as much as his fans." Vaughn gazed back at his phone screen. "Now that I think about it, Nick did become an aerobics star by accident."

Ramona tugged at his sleeve. "We should go, sweetheart. The ice cream will melt."

Vaughn ignored his wife's plea. "Nick was doing background work for one of Barbie's videos. I remember she got violently ill, food poisoning or something, and couldn't perform." He looked at his wife for confirmation. "Isn't that right?"

Ramona had taken a sudden interest in the floor. "Hmm. I don't remember."

Vaughn shrugged. "I had already hired a crew, and Nick knew all the moves, so… I guess the show did go on that time."

Ramona's hand clap signaled her reentry into the conversation. "And it'll go on again." She gripped the cart handle and started to push it away.

"Did you know Nick smoked?" I asked.

"Such a nasty habit." Ramona clicked her tongue. "I'm the one who persuaded him to stop."

"He didn't. He vaped and wore nicotine patches instead." I tilted my head, recalling Trevor's claim that after Ramona confronted Nick over his smoking, she caught him vaping behind the gym—and threatened to fire him. "You must have known," I said to Vaughn. "He used patches when filming. He wore one the day he died."

"Easy enough to edit around." Vaughn stared at the poker game on his phone. "Whatever Nick needed to get the job done in the shortest amount of time. Shame we never got one final video with him."

"What about those solo strength videos you filmed?" I asked. "The ones with Nick using that resistance band?"

Vaughn shook his head. "I'd have to get permission from Marisol to use that footage. Not worth the aggravation."

"Isn't the resistance band your prototype?"

"Hers." Ramona spun the cart around. "Marisol doesn't work for us. She worked for Nick." She pinched her nose. "A bit too hooked on her snow cones, if you catch my drift." She gave one of those slow-motion creepy winks.

I fiddled with the strap of my shopping bag. Marisol's behavior on set indicated she might have been using. Was I acting the same way? Is that why Levi asked about it during my panic attack?

Ramona continued, "Besides, Barbara Lou Sinclair Fitness is a family business, and Marisol is no Sinclair. Life will be much simpler without her or her silly ideas."

"Nick isn't a Sinclair either," Levi said. "He's also gone, but he still makes you money. I supposed that's simpler for you too."

Vaughn's face paled. "What... What do you mean?"

Levi pulled out his phone for reference. "You have an extensive catalog of fitness videos, but the most popular titles featured Nick. Titles like *Belles, Buckaroos, and Burpees.* Viewers rated that one five out of five fist pumps." He pumped the air in demonstration.

"Next was *Fillies, Fellers, and Free Weights* followed by *Dames, Dudes, and Dumbbells—*"

"Yes, yes, I'm familiar." A burst of laughter escaped through Vaughn's pinched lips. "I directed all those, after all."

Levi continued, "*Sheilas, Stallions, and Squats?*"

"Who's Sheila?" I asked.

"It's Australian slang for a young woman," Vaughn said. "It confused a lot of viewers."

"Yes, well, alliteration only takes you so far." Levi stage-whispered to me, "Remind me to show you the picture I found of Odessa Schubert in Lycra and leg warmers."

"Our entire catalog is impressive, Mayor Blue." Ramona's voice was chipper, but the plastic smile had melted down her face. "Viewers benefit from *all* our content."

"But they prefer the stuff with Nick, and Nick makes you money." Levi pocketed his phone. "I bet his surprising and premature death has spiked your sales."

The lines on Vaughn's throat tightened. "I… I wouldn't know."

That surprised me. "Who would?"

"Vaughn, the ice cream," Ramona insisted.

He gave a slight wave before shuffling away.

Chapter 9

WE ARRANGED THE FRUITS AND VEGETABLES into the baskets on our Segways and motored through the town square, toward Levi's mayoral McMansion.

"Vaughn doesn't appear to have much of a motive for killing Nick," Levi said. He'd purchased wireless walkie-talkie headsets so that we could communicate while on the Segways. "But having to work with *and* be related to Barbara Lou would understandably drive anyone over the edge."

I tightened my grip on the handlebars of the two-wheeled contraption. The added heft of the groceries caused me to redistribute my weight. "I don't think that fits the definition of justifiable homicide. Ramona is intense too. I noticed that the other day with the unsettling laugh and the head bobbing."

"Hmm. Do all those tics make for a murderer?"

As an oncoming car passed me, I tensed. "Ramona seemed happy to be rid of Marisol. She was part of Nick's entourage, and we know Nick's smoking was costing the gym business. Perhaps it's a two-birds, one-stone type of scenario. I admit, it's a weak motive for murder."

"And the money the Lone Star makes off Nick's participation in those fitness videos outweighs a few canceled gym memberships."

"Still, your questions about the gym profiting from Nick's death were impressive. You should share those hunches with Monday."

"*Monday*, eh?" Levi said with a grin.

We passed the square's Victorian-era storefronts. The architecture was one of its best features. Multistoried, colorfully painted brick buildings with canted bay windows and turrets lined the area. I gave the Cherry Blossom a nod as we moved past its yellow-and-pink brick exterior and dark-red shutters and trim. Jenny had gotten a great deal on her space, and media coverage of the epic town fraud Levi and I had discovered generated interest in the other storefronts that were for lease. No one had moved in yet, but I predicted Levi's knack for glad-handing prospective shop owners would work in Bluebonnet Hills's favor.

Levi said, "I get the sense that Chief Malone doesn't like me much."

Images of a tween-age Monday swooning over magazine centerfolds of Levi made me chuckle. "Everyone likes you. It's one of your more annoying qualities."

Levi was silent for a moment before gliding into a metered parking spot in front of the courthouse. I pulled in behind him and studied his expression as he ambled toward me.

"What is it?"

"Have you told her?" he asked quietly. "About what's wrong with me?"

"What's wrong? What do you…? Is this about your dad?"

He kicked at the asphalt.

"Nothing's *wrong* with you, Levi. I told you that earlier. You're not your dad, and there's a chance—a very good one—these recent memory lapses are related to stress and change."

Levi pressed his lips into a thin line, his eyes drifting over my shoulder.

"And to answer your question, no. I don't share what we discuss with anyone, including with Jenny. That's your news to share." I swallowed. "That said, you're the mayor now. Perhaps confiding in the police chief would be a responsible thing to do."

Levi continued to avoid eye contact. "Remind me what we know about Celeste and Nick going to church."

I shook my head to absorb the tsunami of randomness flowing out of Levi. "Uh, well, Barbara Lou said Celeste was interested in Nick. Romantically." I recalled the conversation at the café. "Monday mentioned that Nick wore a St. Benito charm. He protects you from disease and promotes health. Perhaps Nick wore it for symbolic reasons rather than for religious ones."

Levi flinched. "Chief Malone shared this?"

"She mentioned the charm." I adjusted my shirt collar. "I researched St. Benito."

"Sounds like you've been investigating on your own." His shoulders drooped, and he stepped back toward the Segway. "You'll have to tell me what other information you two exchanged."

"We didn't exchange—"

Levi held his hand in the air. "Turn around."

Celeste and Marisol stood on the steps outside the Methodist church, talking to Monday, who had her back to us. Her head was down as she focused on the notepad in her hands.

Marisol gestured wildly. She wore a low-cut sundress and stiletto heels. She'd piled her hair onto her head and fastened it with a metal clip. Even from across the street, I could make out Celeste's thickly painted eyebrows, which arched in response to whatever Monday was asking. I glanced at the clock on my phone. A Tuesday afternoon at three fifteen didn't seem like a churchgoing time. And Celeste and Marisol were a mismatched pair of parishioners. Were they there together, mourning Nick?

A few moments later, Monday closed her notebook, handed each woman a card, and hustled toward her cruiser. When she was out of earshot, Marisol restarted her wild gesticulation, prompting Celeste to check her wristwatch.

Levi spun the Segway around and headed toward the church.

"What are you doing?" I asked into the microphone of my walkie-talkie.

"Detecting." Levi decelerated to keep pace with Marisol, who clacked her stilettos down the sidewalk.

I leaned forward and followed. Celeste, her arms crossed, watched me pass her on the church's steps.

"EXCUSE ME, MADEMOISELLE," Levi said. "We're with the Bluebonnet Hills Beautification Society. May we ask you a few questions about the landscape of our wonderful town square?"

"You're the bozos from the fitness shoot." Marisol's heels clicked as she strolled toward Levi's Segway. "And aren't you the mayor?"

"I wear many hats. I'm Mayor Levi Blue, and this is my associate, Deputy Sho 'No Mercy' Tanaka."

Yes, we would be revisiting my "cool" new name.

Marisol stopped to adjust the strap of her handbag, which appeared to be weighing her down. "Is this some kind of low-speed chase, then?" She glanced at our groceries. "Or do you just travel around selling produce?"

"I have some bok choy I'd part with," Levi said. "But we were worried about you after you left the shoot. No one could find you."

"Here I am!" Marisol covered her eyes with her hands and flailed her arms at us. "Boo, bozos."

Levi and I both flinched at the theatrics, the intended effect of Marisol's demented version of peekaboo, as her cackle suggested.

"It's been real," she said. "Unless you've got an organic mango in your traveling fruit basket, I've got a schedule to keep."

"Leaving town?" I called after her, causing her to stop and face me. "With Nick gone, I suppose there isn't much keeping you here. Unless the police still have questions for you."

"Is that Hello Kitty?" Marisol pointed at the decal of the cartoon cat with a red bow plastered on my helmet. "I'm not under arrest, nosy. I can leave town when I want. And not that it's any of your business, but I have other opportunities to explore here in Petticoat Junction before I leave."

"What exactly does an influencer do?" Levi asked. "Is that like an image consultant? I worked with PR people on *Tween of the Crime*, and I was thinking an image consultant might help me promote some of my mayoral initiatives to the residents here."

Marisol studied Levi before digging a hand into her oversized purse and revealing a business card. "I'm not an *influencer*." She handed Levi the card. "Influencers are Kewpie-doll socialites scavenging for free makeup and hair products to demo on their vapid social channels. I'm a digital-content strategist. I use analytics, actual data, to drive traffic to meaningful content."

"Did Nick provide meaningful content?" I asked. "You were working for him."

"We had an arrangement, yeah." Marisol chuckled. "He had a killer smile, a smoking bod, and some fitness knowledge but zero brand identity. That's where I came in. He was wasting his time here, clomping around with a herd of middle-aged biggins in animal-print leotards."

I tightened my grip around the handlebars. Marisol had an intensity that was both exciting and frightening. "Nick was planning to leave the Lone Star? To venture out on his own?"

Marisol dug into her bag again and pulled out the lilac chain-length resistance band Nick had used during our fitness shoot. "It's just a prototype but pretty close to the finished product." She expanded and retracted the band. "The market for at-home fitness content is insane. If you can create that content and add in some modestly priced equipment, well, you're making some serious bank."

I asked, "So you were creating fitness content with Nick using your products?"

"I would have made both of us a lot of money. But of course, Nick came with his baggage, with his conditions." She gave Levi a cursory glance. "Typical diva."

"What kinds of conditions?" he asked. "Did he want you to buy the spring where all his special water came from?"

Marisol snorted. "He agreed to leave the Lone Star if I created something for crazy-eyed Barbara Lou. I mean, create what? *Sweatin' with the Oldie*? No, thanks."

"Hold on," Levi said. "Nick wanted to help Barbara Lou? Why? And she owns all the Lone Star content. She has no reason to leave."

"*Co*-owns," Marisol clarified. "With that wet-blanket brother. Don't get me started on all that 'We're a family business' nonsense. Anyway, she wasn't leaving the Lone Star, just doing some side projects with me."

"What were Vaughn's objections?" I asked.

"He was worried it would mess with Barbara Lou's image. And I respected that. I mean, at least the dude understands branding. But we're targeting two different markets. I want fresh and edgy."

"How fresh and edgy were you going to make Barbara Lou?" Levi asked with a shiver.

"Oh, man, you should have heard the things she pitched." Marisol cackled. "I think my favorite concept was *Strippin' with the Oldie*."

"Strippin'… Uh. What is that exactly?"

"Strip aerobics. It's a combination of striptease techniques with aerobic moves. *That*, I can market, but not starring Barbara Lou. I mean, there's probably a niche market there, but I don't deal in fetish fitness."

"So that's where the negotiations halted?" I asked. "With Nick? With the Sinclair siblings?"

Marisol narrowed her eyes. "We were just getting started, as I had suspected. This wasn't about 'brand' or 'family.' Vaughn wanted money. Desperately. So I propositioned him." She quirked the corner of her mouth and raised the resistance band. "Vaughn agreed to shoot a few solo videos with this little moneymaker and Nick—my other little moneymaker. He'd edit and score every-thing, and we'd co-own the content. I'd sign an exclusive—but short-term—contract to sell these bands at the Lone Star, and we'd split the profits."

"That seems like a reasonable deal." But of course, I didn't know what a reasonable deal was.

Marisol shrugged. "I thought so, but Vaughn got back on his high horse again, spouting that 'family business' blah blah."

"He got a conscience? Felt like a sellout?"

"No, dummy, he wanted more money. I told him, let's start slow, stay on first base. If things trended in the direction I'd predicted, well, I agreed to buy Vaughn out."

Levi and I exchanged shocked expressions. "Buy Vaughn out of the Lone Star? What would you gain from that?"

Marisol jutted her chin and let the resistance band dangle to one side. "Dude's got like three decades' worth of content that's already produced and edited. If I got ahold of all that, I could consolidate it onto a single streaming platform. Devise a nice little subscription model."

"I suppose Nick's death thwarts that idea."

Marisol focused on me. "Do you underestimate everyone or just women?"

"I… uh…"

She dismissed me with a wave. "Like I already told you, I've still got some business here." Glaring in the church's direction, she said, "Besides, Celeste is holding my phone hostage."

I followed her line of vision. "Are you and Celeste good friends?"

Marisol laughed. "She's just playing another stupid game. But I need that phone. It's got all the videos I shot of Nick using the resistance band. I never got to post them, and his fans are probably dying to see them."

"No pun intended, right?" I asked.

"Me-ow." Marisol swiped the air with her hand. "Hello Kitty likes to scratch."

I snickered. She was certainly clever. "I'm curious. All this added aggravation with managing Barbara Lou, with dealing with Vaughn—was Nick worth all that?"

Marisol gazed behind us. "Eh, Nick was a world-class jerk, but he connected with the camera in ways you can't teach. I could've easily found other guys, hotter ones with whiter teeth and bigger muscles, but Nick didn't require as much effort. And, well, throw in a sizable content sample, and I could build a platform and grow it the way I wanted."

I considered that. "Were you and Nick, uh… involved?"

"Would you ask a man that question?"

My jaw dropped a little. "I… Er, it's only that Nick said he had recently broken up with his girlfriend. Levi and I hoped she might have some information."

"Nick and I were strictly professional. I didn't want to go anywhere near that. His relationship with Psycho Eyes was enough to turn anyone off."

"With Barbara Lou, you mean?"

"Their relationship, it was just strange. Obsessive, even. I caught Barbara Lou in Nick's bathroom one day. She was digging through his trash, putting stuff into little plastic bags."

"What kind of stuff?" I asked.

"Like those Q-Tips. You know, what you use to clean your ears? Disgusting. Creepy."

"I'll say," I replied.

Marisol chuckled, her laser focus back on me. "Here, Rum Tum Tugger." She held out the resistance band. "I'm all out of catnip, so here's a toy to entertain you. Seems like you got some pent-up frustrations you haven't been able to take out on your scratching post. Try this."

I took the resistance band, mumbled a thank-you, and dropped it into my basket.

Marisol hoisted the strap of her bag on her shoulder. "No need to thank me. I don't want to find any dead mice outside my door tomorrow."

As she walked away, Levi fanned himself. "She's intense."

Intense was one word for it. I glanced back at the church and thought I understood why Celeste, Marisol, and Nick were regular attendees.

Chapter 10

"I'M CELESTE. I'M AN ADDICT."

"Hi, Celeste," the audience chorused.

I'd crumpled into a metal folding chair at the back of the church basement. After I'd reflected on my conversation with Celeste at the aerobics shoot and our afternoon encounter with Marisol, it took only a few internet clicks to learn the Methodist church hosted the town's Narcotics Anonymous meetings.

Celeste began, "We lost a friend this week. Some of you didn't know Nick. Others of you knew him too well."

The audience chuckled.

"Nick was a good person. Imperfect, flawed, human. But good.

And tonight, I'm asking myself a lot of questions and wondering why I'm able to stand up here and not Nick.

"I was supposed to be a star. And at one point in my life, nothing was telling me I wouldn't be. My childhood was decent, and I had an education and had been in love." She laughed. "Many, *many* times over. But it was never enough. I wanted more. And I wanted what you had. Then even that wasn't enough."

Celeste touched her hair, which she'd spiked, giving it the shape and color of an Easter chick.

"My star burned out and exploded before I knew what was happening. I'd never felt that sense of loss before, never experienced that depth of failure. Naturally, I reacted the way any self-respecting small-town gal would. I got high. After I lost a few more jobs, I wised up enough to know my recreational drug use was becoming a habit. I also convinced myself I could get it under control." Celeste held one hand out and placed the other on her hip. "I'd be okay if I learned to smoke meth socially—like a lady."

The audience erupted in laughter, and a few clapped. I even caught myself smiling and my shoulders relaxing.

Celeste tugged at her royal-blue scarf. Wearing that color appeared to boost her confidence. "I also convinced myself I was invincible, because that's what drugs do. Then I wrapped my car around a live oak." She cocked her head to one side. "The tree's still standing. A little broken, a little scarred, but I pass it whenever I come to town. I've overcome a lot of denials and gone through physical therapy and surgeries, including the one that botched my face."

Celeste looked down to compose her thoughts. "I'm at peace with the imperfect, flawed human I've become. Hell, I'm glad to be here, period. If fentanyl were as easy to get back then as it is now, I would have OD'd before I could face off with that oak tree. I am here tonight, fifteen years clean, thank God"—she pointed heavenward—"but the urge to use again has never been stronger."

The fluorescent lighting illuminated the tears in her eyes. "I want answers for Nick. Selfishly, I need answers for myself. I was his sponsor. For crying out loud, I was standing right there when he—"

Celeste inhaled deeply, and her eyes drifted to the back of the room. Her gaze landed on me, and she gave a thin smile of recognition.

"But answers won't satisfy me," she said. "And that's this crazy merry-go-round we call addiction, right? I want what I want. And I want what you have. But nothing will help this make sense. I hope sharing with you now helps me keep perspective on what I *do* have." She swallowed. "We have several phrases around here, but we repeat them because they're the truth. I've been repeating one to myself today: 'Keep coming back. It works.' Thank you."

The attendees offered Celeste a round of appreciative applause, but the meeting moved quickly into the next share. I counted about forty people, an even mix of Bluebonnet Hills residents and people from neighboring towns, and was surprised by how many people I knew by name or face. In fact, one attendee seemed so out of place that it made my jaw go slack. I repositioned myself behind the person in front of me to avoid an awkward interaction.

At the end of the meeting, everyone stood and recited the Twelfth Tradition. We all proceeded to the back of the room to feast on burned coffee and doughnuts that tasted like the oil they'd been fried in. I'd have put money in the donation basket, but I never carried cash. I retreated farther into the corner, and attendees filed past me on their way to the refreshment table, nodding at the semi-familiar faces and avoiding eye contact with the more familiar faces. I turned away, bumping into someone.

"Monday? Er, Chief Malone? Hello."

Monday wore her wheat-colored hair down, which was why I'd missed her when scanning the audience. "Tanaka? I didn't... Uh, howdy there."

"I arrived late, so I slipped in the back. Your hair. It's down."

She shrugged. "Off duty."

"It's beautiful. Or nice. I mean, it's nice if you like hair."

"I'm kinda partial to mine, so… thank you? So…"

"So…"

Monday pointed at herself. "I'm not a… if that's what you're thinking. My sister was… still *is*, I think. I don't know where she is now. I started attending meetings when I was a detective in Lubbock. Listening to other people's stories helps me. Makes me less angry at January."

"What's wrong with January?" I scrunched my mouth in concentration. "Oh, that's your sister's name? Huh. January and Monday Malone. The beginning of every year and every week."

Monday shook her head, unamused. "Heard it all before, buster." Her forest-green eyes sparkled a little when she laughed. "What are you doing here? Sorry, I shouldn't ask that."

"It's all right. I came here on a hunch. Almost chickened out."

Monday's eyes narrowed. "Tanaka, you're smarter than this." She gripped the sleeve of my blazer and tugged me toward a corner. "You're investigating Nick's murder, aren't you? This is NA. You can't be here digging for clues." She stopped to survey my scowl. "Oh, no. Where's Levi? Where's your dingus in crime?" Monday slouched and peered under a row of folding chairs. "He won't leap out from under here, will he?" She tightened her grip and jerked her head around the room. "Dear Lord, don't tell me he's around here. In disguise."

I shook out of her grip and smoothed the fabric. "Levi isn't here." I gritted my teeth. "And he doesn't know I'm here."

"Oh." She tried to smooth where she'd grabbed my blazer. "Bluebonnet Hills must seem mighty boring to a Seattle guy like you. You're probably going a little stir crazy. I mean, if I hung around with Mayor McCheesy all the time, I'd gouge my peepers out with a rusty spoon."

"Your peepers?"

She gave an exasperated sigh. "But *I* love boring. Know why? Boring means no murder. That's one reason I took this job."

"Isn't Lubbock a college town?" I asked. "You break up a lot of bar fights among the frat houses while you were there?"

"Cute." Monday's jaw twitched. "Not many bar fights. Some foot pursuits, vehicle pursuits, armed robbery, and I've been shot at once or twice. I also experienced what Miz Gravell shared about tonight. Drug addiction infects a lot of our Texas towns. Crack, heroin, meth. Serious stuff."

I swept my hand through my hair. "When I'm nervous, I make glib statements."

"Tanaka, this isn't *Murder, She Wrote*. Don't make me give the 'Stay out of my investigation' sermon." She shook her head. "You can't just pedal your two-wheelie thingamajig around town, hunting for clues."

I adjusted the lapels of my jacket. "Segways are electric transportation. No pedals." I lowered my voice to a growl. "And believe me, I have no interest in getting involved—"

"Evening, y'all." Celeste's voice ended our conversation and caused Monday and me to jump. I might also have yelped.

"Miz Gravell, evening." Monday's face reddened. "Your share was mighty powerful. You're right about fentanyl—it's poisoning our state. In my officer duties, responding to overdoses is not a pleasant experience. Especially when it's a young person. Watching a kid die from an OD hit me hard."

"I'm sorry to hear that." Celeste assessed the chief with a tilt of her head. "Did my share gain any new leads about Nick's death? That's really why you're here, yes?"

Monday's eyes darted around the room. She stepped closer to Celeste and lowered her voice. "Miz Gravell, I assure you, I mean no disrespect."

"Everyone is welcome, Chief. Though considering you

questioned me here earlier about Nick, you'll forgive me if I'm a tad… suspicious."

Monday, a peacekeeper, held out her hands. "I just came tonight to listen. If you want to talk about Nick or you remember anything new, just lemme know. If you don't feel comfortable at the station, we can grab a coffee." She motioned to the coffee urn the meeting's attendees were draining. "We can grab a cup now, if you'd like."

"I don't think so, Chief." Celeste made eye contact with me. "Good to see you here, Sho."

I nodded in greeting but stared at my shoes. They wept for a shine.

"Sho is my coffee date tonight," Celeste continued. "I have your card, Chief. I'll call if I change my mind."

"Much obliged, Miz Gravell. Again, I apologize if my presence gave you the wrong impression. I appreciated your share." She turned toward me but looked down. Perhaps she noticed my shoes too. "'Night, Tanaka," she said before rushing out the door.

"Are you two together?" Celeste asked me.

I pointed behind me. "With Monday?" I gave a nervous laugh. "No, we just ran into each other."

Celeste arched a thick eyebrow. "Interesting. I watched you two from across the room. Sensed a little sizzle there."

"Sizzle? I'm more sputter and spit. You've seen my aerobics moves."

"You've got smoother moves than you think," she said. "You need to relax. Get out of your head."

"You sound like my sister… and Levi."

"Both incredibly wise people." Her eyes crinkled when she smiled, which were the only wrinkles on her face. "Is that why you came tonight? To learn how to get out of your head?"

I removed my blazer and laid it over the back of a folding chair. The church basement was getting hot. "Curious, I guess."

"Curious about Nick's murder or curious about how to begin your recovery?"

"Both, perhaps. How did you know?"

"That you're an addict?"

I darted my eyes around the room.

Celeste laughed. "Relax, Sho. They're all addicts too. And the truth is I didn't know. I suspected, but my intuition's been wrong before."

"Actually, I don't believe I'm an addict. I mean, perhaps I was, for a very short period, addicted to prescription medication. But that's all over now."

Celeste nodded. "That's wonderful to hear. How'd you make it through? Rehab? Therapy?"

I shook my head. "Therapy was too woo-woo for me."

"So you attended regular meetings back home? Where is that again?"

"Seattle, and this is only my second meeting. I attended the first as part of my nursing education."

"You've beaten your addiction, then? That's what you said? The urge to use is completely erased?"

I swallowed. "Not exactly, no. I think about using every day. Multiple times a day."

"You're in the right place. 'Keep coming back. It works.'" She slapped her thighs. "You want coffee?"

"Any tea?"

"We've got tepid water and a generic brand of tea bags."

I laughed. "That'll get the job done."

Celeste extended an arm. "Pop a squat. I'll grab your tea, and we can chat."

SITTING ACROSS FROM CELESTE, I played with the string of my

tea bag and stared at the wall just above her shoulder. If I made eye contact, I would lose my nerve.

I began, "Several months ago, a domestic-abuse survivor arrived in my Seattle ICU with a brain injury. She had been escaping an ex and swerved her car into oncoming traffic. Struck by an eighteen-wheeler."

"And she survived? Heavens. All I hit was a tree." Celeste brushed her fingers against her collarbone. "Continue, please."

"One night, during my rounds, the ex-husband showed up. He'd brought a gun or what I thought was one. It was actually a toy, but I learned that after throwing myself on the patient." I shifted in my seat and rubbed at the pain in my lower back. "When I discovered the gun was a toy, I slapped the guy around with it. Two orderlies had to lift me off him."

Celeste laughed in mid-sip of her coffee. "In Texas, we call that a pistol whipping." She rubbed a finger over her likely burned lips. "And that triggered the addiction?"

"I'd never experienced that level of rage before. Or since." As I gripped my cup, my fingers dimpled into the sides. "Besides the anger, I felt nervousness and paranoia. Every sound in that ICU made me jump, from the beeps of the heart rate monitors to the elevator lurches. And that patient's room. I couldn't stand going in there again."

"Understandably. It made you relive the trauma."

"It wasn't only that." I blinked back into focus and looked at Celeste. "It was the patient. She thanked me every time she saw me. I got physically ill when she squeezed my hand." I blew air out through my nose. "Shielding her in the way I did, I... I could have caused her greater damage."

"You just heard me share my vices. What about you? What's your drug of choice?"

"I initially resisted the suggestion of medication. No one understood the damaging effects of benzos and opioids more than I did. Still, the hospital psychiatrist insisted. She wanted to keep the licensing board happy. Antidepressants seemed like the safest choice. Zoloft gave me this… floaty feeling. I glided above any conflict like I was watching a movie starring someone who resembled me. That nagging inner voice disappeared, the one that pushed me to work more hours, to make more money, and to ignore those monthly catchups with my sister. If you'd known me then, before the incident, before the drugs, you'd understand how driven I was. High-strung, perhaps. It felt good not to care. I got addicted to that feeling."

I recognized my voice, but the words sounded strange. *Did I just confess to being addicted?*

Celeste said, "I suppose you had access to all kinds of stuff. ICUs sound like candy stores to a reformed junkie like me." She leaned forward. "Did you take medication from your patients?"

"The temptation was there, but no. When the dosage the psychiatrist prescribed wasn't enough, I asked a colleague for help—a bold move, one I couldn't keep trying, or…"

"Risk being outed?"

"It felt sleazy to ask colleagues for drugs. Strangely, I had no remorse swiping prescription pads from my unit and forging myself into an addiction."

I'd said it again—addiction.

"Are you taking antidepressants now?" Celeste asked.

"I relapsed—briefly—after arriving in Bluebonnet Hills." The tea was tepid, but my throat welcomed the moisture. "After my hospital placed me on leave, I vowed to taper off Zoloft. I thought I could handle it myself. Still do." I shrugged. "I'm past the worst part—dizziness, nausea, tingling skin. Now it's mood swings and extra glugs of red wine."

"Less Zoloft but more merlot."

"I've tried to hide everything from Jenny, but… she's annoy-ingly perceptive."

Did all that tumble from my mouth? In a moldy church basement, sipping expired tea, confiding in someone I barely know?

Perhaps if I stayed frozen, Celeste would forget I was there. Or perhaps she would choke on her laughter or stand up and announce that I was not only helpless but also a lost cause. I pictured the next day's lead headline in the *Bluebonnet Bee.*

"Thank you for trusting me," Celeste said after a momentary silence. "You've made a huge first step toward recovery. I hope you see that."

I wished I could wipe away the entire exchange. "In your share, you mentioned wanting to be a star. When we spoke to Barbara Lou, she referenced a falling out. Are those two things connected?"

"Big Louie strikes again." Celeste crossed her legs. "Sorry, that was my former mean-girl talking."

Grinning, I asked, "Who's Big Louie?"

"A nickname someone gave Barbie in high school." She slapped her knee. "Okay, *I* gave her that nickname. But we've made amends. She became a fitness mentor."

"Were you in her early videos?" The Schubert sisters had mentioned Barbara Lou's first videos featured the residents of Bluebonnet Hills.

"I started as a background player… and fell in love. That changed everything between me and Barbie." Celeste cocked an eyebrow. "The man I married? It was Vaughn."

I did a double take. "Did he seduce you with his phone holster?"

"Blessedly, this was way before cell phones." She laughed. "Vaughn has always directed Barbie's videos, so he gave me little bits to do here and there. Those little bits got bigger, and Vaughn convinced us to shoot a video together."

"I… I don't remember hearing that title when Levi read them off the website."

"You wouldn't have. Vaughn branded us the Gal Pals of Fitness." Celeste rolled her eyes. "He thought women would find exercising together motivating."

"Barbara Lou didn't like that concept?"

"She loved it. Said it was just about the best idea ever," Celeste said in a mocking voice. "Plastered on a big old toothy smile and hugged me."

"What happened?"

Celeste tilted her head, clearly calculating how much to say. "I think Barbie slipped me a laxative."

I almost spilled my tea. "She what?"

"We used to take laxatives to control our weight and look less puffy on camera." Celeste glanced over her shoulder. "I can't prove it, but after I drank my water, I got too sick to perform."

"Your water…" I considered that. "I'm sure Vaughn hated to cancel the shoot."

"You know how quirky Vaughn is about his schedules and his budgets. He hasn't changed much." She shook her head. "Barbie shot the video solo. As always."

"Like she wanted."

Celeste sipped her coffee and sat back. "The video was popular, surprise, surprise. I wouldn't have added anything to it."

"Still, I can't imagine working with Barbara Lou after all that."

"It's not the worst thing she's ever done to me. And a perk from sticking by her for so long is watching karma come around. And boy, did it bite Barbie right in that big old flabby butt of hers." Celeste mimed pouring something into her coffee cup.

I gasped. "You mean, you spiked her water?"

Waving a hand, Celeste said, "I wish I could take credit for that."

"Nick?"

She stared at the ceiling. "Maybe. It was during the video that got Nicky out of the background and alongside Barbie. But he would have told me. He didn't keep many secrets from me. At least, I don't think he did."

I smoothed the fabric of my pants legs. "Forgive me for prying, but Nick and Barbara Lou appeared to have a… complex relationship."

"Complex is a good word for it." She grinned. "Unless you're implying those two were a romantic item."

"Were they?"

Celeste appeared to consider. "There was a closeness between them, definitely, but Barbie was more maternal than anything." She crossed her legs. "Nicky got quite a makeover when he arrived in town. You wouldn't have recognized him—he was gaunt, jittery, with these wide, haunted eyes. And he smelled. Reminded me of old, dry clay." Celeste shivered. "But Barbie saw something in Nick no one else did, including me. She cleaned him up and helped him use fitness as a path to recovery." She laughed. "Barbie saved his life."

"Why did she help Nick? What did she see in him?"

Celeste sighed. "She's certainly experienced tragedy. Mostly self-inflicted, though, if you ask me."

"Petty high school stuff?"

"Barbie and I had a rivalry of sorts." Celeste scraped a foot under the chair. "Before Vaughn, I was married to my high school sweetheart. Pablo Alvarado. Picture your stereotypical all-American football star. Of course, there was more to him than that."

"Did Barbara Lou date him too?" Growing up with my sister, I was all too familiar with the daily angst of high school girls.

"Barbara Lou would tell you Pablo was leaving me for her. At least, that's what she told everyone in town, including the police."

"The police?"

"At the end of his junior year, Pablo suffered a knee injury. He was out for the next season, and his scholarship opportunities dried up. The depression overwhelmed him, and a few years later, he took his own life. Allegedly."

I leaned in. *Allegedly?*

Celeste continued, "Pablo died of an opioid overdose." She stopped to collect her thoughts. "Let me clarify: the autopsy revealed opioids in his system. I don't think he ingested them voluntarily."

"He didn't develop a drug dependency after his football injury?"

"It's a convenient lie." Celeste scrunched her mouth. "I knew my husband. He had a lot of demons." Her eyes watered. "Drugs weren't one of them. And after snowballing down that hill myself, I believe it even more today. I would have known if Pablo was using. Or having an affair." She laughed. "With Barbie, of all people."

"Did Barbara Lou provide proof for any of this?"

Stone-faced, Celeste replied, "She claimed she was pregnant."

I leaned back to catch a breath. "Was she?"

"We nicknamed her Big Louie for a reason. She disappeared that summer. Came back all peppy, a little thinner, and focused on health and fitness. She and Vaughn opened the gym the following year."

I studied the gaps in the basement's flooring. "She rose from the ashes. Just like Nick."

"I'd never considered that, but yeah, maybe that's what she saw in Nick. Herself."

"Marrying Vaughn couldn't have improved your dynamic with Barbara Lou."

"Vaughn and Pablo were best friends in high school. And of course, Ramona was Pablo's little sister."

"Wait." I set down my tea. "Your first husband had an alleged affair with Barbara Lou and was also Ramona's brother? Your second husband is Barbara Lou's brother and is now married to Ramona?"

"It's a small town." Celeste shrugged.

"Ever consider a day trip to Austin? Meet some new people?"

"Bluebonnet Hills could widen its gene pool. But our recent revitalization has brought some great people here, including you and your sister." She set down her coffee and took my hands. "And a support system is an important part of recovery."

"I haven't even told Jenny why I'm on leave from the hospital."

"What about Levi?"

"He knows, but I've only known him a few months."

"Really? When I watch you two interact, you seem like childhood friends."

I chuckled. "I suppose we keep each other's secrets."

"Believe me—good friends are hard to find. If they're already there for you in the worst times, you'll never wonder whether they'll be there during the best."

"You were a good friend to Nick. I can tell." I gently tugged my hands from her hold and rubbed my sweaty palms on my legs.

"Being his sponsor in a small town had its challenges," she said. "Barbie understood my relationship with Nick, but it didn't stop her from telling everyone we were lovers."

I reached for my tea, trying to conceal my red cheeks. No reason to confirm Celeste's suspicions. "Barbara Lou seems possessive, at least regarding Nick. How did she react to his smoking?"

"Now you're investigating." Celeste wagged her finger but smiled. "Nicky was dealing with a tremendous amount of guilt. Fitness replaced his drug addiction, but something else was driving the smoking." She stopped and inhaled deeply through her nose. "Barbie was mostly concerned with Barbie. Surprise. She worried the smoking would hurt her image." Celeste tugged at the knot in her scarf, perhaps recalling the confrontation over her glittery sweatband. "If she'd caught Nick smoking, it wouldn't be the nicotine that killed him."

Barbara Lou was a vending machine stocked with dramatic statements—anyone could pull the lever and see what shot out. Yet a chain-smoking costar would have tarnished her professional reputation. Earlier, the Schubert sisters had confirmed Barbara Lou's brand consciousness. "Nick wore nicotine patches during fitness shoots. Vaughn knew this but could edit around it. Did Barbara Lou?"

"Nicky loved his tank tops, so there weren't many places to hide a patch. He stuck one on his chest once, and Barbie about ripped it off." Celeste winced. "Nicky wised up and moved them to his back. The camera still noticed, but Barbie didn't appear to."

Barbara Lou murdering Nick over a nicotine habit seemed extreme, but so was Barbara Lou. Yet something else poked my brain for attention, something Celeste had said during her share.

If fentanyl was as easy to get back then as it is now, I would have OD'd before I could face off with that oak tree.

After a hasty but appreciative goodbye to Celeste, I ran up the stairs of the basement and practically leaped down the outside church steps. As I clutched my phone, my fingers hovered over Levi's number.

Then I stopped, scrolled through my contacts, and made another call instead.

Chapter 11

I PULLED THE SEGWAY into the Lone Star the next morning, feeling refreshed despite a lack of sleep. Even Ojii-chan's tracksuit smelled clean, thanks to Jenny's washing.

Levi opened the door wearing a lopsided grin. And that ridiculously perfect outfit.

"We're in the other studio today?" I asked.

Levi slapped me on the back. "Let's hit it." He led the way to the Tumbleweed Room, which was about half the size of the original studio.

Tallulah, the Brussels griffon, shot out from somewhere and ran to Levi, who scooped her up and began petting her.

Celeste followed with a wave. "She was hoping you'd come back," she said to Levi, who was already feeding the dog bacon.

"I would never leave my wittle girl Wulah," Levi baby-talked.

"Only a few of us today." Celeste leaned toward me. "Less of us to focus on, so less time for screw-ups."

Tingly heat brushed across my brow.

"Relax." Celeste squeezed my wrist. "Barbie's routines move at a gentler pace, and she repeats a lot of her moves. You'll be fine."

Barbara Lou bounced through the studio door, bedazzled like a disco ball. Sequins were placed within her helmet hair, her eyelashes caked with so much mascara that her naturally bug eyes looked even more alert.

"The fitness queen reclaims her throne," Celeste said.

"Vaughn?" Barbara Lou slapped the pages of her script against her palm. "I have notes."

Marisol followed Barbara Lou, her oversize handbag slung over her shoulder, and wildly texted with both thumbs.

"And Marisol is her lady-in-waiting?" I asked. "That's unexpected."

Celeste's cheeks reddened. "Marisol's always lying in wait, always hungry for opportunity." She raised a fist and shook it. "With Nicky gone, she's got to get that fix somewhere."

"I woke up inspired this morning," Barbara Lou chirped at her brother.

Vaughn's head and shoulders slumped so that he looked anything but inspired.

"I want our fans to feel empowered by this new routine," Barbara Lou continued. "We need a new title as well. Something like *Heroines and High Knees* or *Goddesses and Glutes*."

"Ooh, love, love, love those." Marisol adjusted some sequins in Barbara Lou's hair. "So fierce."

"Uh… We can certainly consider those," Vaughn said to the floor.

"Now, about the fly-over shots for the knee lifts." Barbara Lou stabbed her finger into the script, which didn't seem to awaken Vaughn's enthusiasm. "I want the camera on me first. Make sure you get the movement of my hands touching my knee. Then pull away and show the rest of the group."

"Same shot we always do," Vaughn said.

Marisol stepped back to admire Barbara Lou, her manicured finger tapping her chin. "Something's missing." She waved her hands excitedly. "Jewelry!"

Barbara Lou rolled her head toward Marisol. "You don't wear jewelry in a fitness shoot, dear." She laughed to disguise the annoyance in her voice. "Bless your heart."

"Something else, then." Marisol snapped her fingers. "Where's the seamstress?"

Vaughn muttered and returned to his expectant group of unpaid interns.

Ramona inched into view. "Do you mean me?"

"We need *something* here." Marisol waved a hand over Barbara Lou. "She's the star. She needs to look it." Marisol removed a giant can of hair spray from her purse.

"She's already quite, uh, sparkly. Does she need more?"

"What about those jewel-encrusted sweatbands I gave you?" Marisol oscillated the hairspray can around Barbara Lou like she was dusting crops. "Those samples? That you never used?"

"We… We still have those. Somewhere." Ramona swallowed. "Probably in the storeroom."

Marisol shot Ramona an over-the-shoulder glare. "They won't unpack themselves."

Ramona scurried away, bumping into Trevor, who bounded toward us wearing a safety-cone-orange tank top.

"Look, Mayor Blue. Mr. Vaughn made me a background player. Check out my moves." Trevor raised his arms and shimmied with a wide smile. "Super cool, huh?"

Levi wiped his eyes. "I have nothing left to teach you."

"No hooting and hollering today, boys." Celeste fixed her glare on Marisol and Barbara Lou. "This is a one-woman show. Stand in the back, smile, and follow her lead."

Vaughn called over his shoulder, "You want a rehearsal, Barbie? Everyone is here."

Barbara Lou shoved her script into Marisol's hands and strutted to the set. "Let's begin with the opening."

Vaughn clapped. "Places, everyone. Remember, big smiles throughout." His eyes flicked in my direction. "Look like you're happy to be here, not like someone murdered your dog."

Levi pulled Lulah closer and massaged the rolls in her neck.

"Always the wordsmith." Celeste clicked her tongue and gently pulled the dog from Levi's hold. "I'll move Miss Lulah to her bed. Save me a spot in the back, boys."

As Levi and I made our way to the back of the set, Barbara Lou did a few head rolls and shook the nerves out of her hands. "Gimme a countdown, will you, Vaughn?"

Celeste darted back onto the set and between Levi and me. "And three… two…"

Barbara Lou popped to attention like a newly possessed marionette. "Howdy! Y'all ready to lasso those extra pounds and put 'em out to—"

"Found it!" Ramona bolted back into the room, waving a sparkling white sweatband.

"Stop!" Vaughn called.

Marisol tugged the sweatband from Ramona's hand and gave a disgusted sigh. "Pink would have been better."

"Sorry." Ramona pushed against the door. "I can go back and look."

"Forget it." Marisol strode onto the set, the white sweatband draped across her hands like she was crowning a queen.

Barbara Lou bent her knees and bowed her head.

"Do you see this?" I asked Levi through clenched teeth. "She literally curtsied."

"Anytime you're ready." The tone in Vaughn's voice suggested he shared my disbelief.

"It's still not quite right." Marisol pouted. "It's the hair. Needs to be even bigger, a little more lift at the roots."

"This is ridiculous." Celeste elbowed me. "That hair already needs a separate studio."

I rubbed the goose bumps forming on my arms. "There's certainly a distinct energy here compared to the first shoot."

"Barbie, girl, where's your teasing brush?" Marisol walked to where Barbara Lou had flung her duffel bag.

"We can't stop between every take to tease your hair," Vaughn said.

"Getting the details perfect, brother dear. You can appreciate… Nooo!" Barbara Lou delivered a scream only rivaled by the one Marisol simultaneously released.

Marisol dangled a plastic bag between her fingers. Revolted, she tossed the bag into the middle of the room.

I crouched to inspect the black clumps in the bag. "Is that hair? What's that doing in Barbara Lou's duffel?"

"Good morning, everybody. Sorry to interrupt." Chief Malone, flanked by Officers Perkins and Whales, marched into the studio.

"What's going on here?" Vaughn's voice rose. "We're in the middle of a rehearsal, Chief. Can't this wait?"

"No, sir, it cannot." Monday focused on Barbara Lou. "Miz Sinclair, I have a few more questions regarding the murder of Nick Batista. I'd like to invite you down to the station."

Celeste staggered into me, I assumed from the shock of the official announcement of Nick's murder. I wrapped my arm around her shoulders, Levi put his around her waist, and we held her close.

"Is she under arrest?" Vaughn charged toward Monday, causing Officer Perkins to take a step around the chief.

"You're not under arrest, Miz Sinclair. Just have a few questions for ya. If you come with us to the station now, we can clear everything up, and I'll get you back here for your rehearsal."

"Chief?" Officer Whales bent over to retrieve the plastic bag Marisol had tossed.

Monday examined it. "This your hair, Miz Sinclair?"

Barbara Lou scoffed. "Of course not. My hair is curly. And brown."

"True, it's short hair. Black. Kinda like Nick Batista's. Again, Miz Sinclair, I'd like to ask you to come down to the station with us. Now. No handcuffs, just talking."

"This is ridiculous," Barbara Lou said. "I have a perfectly reasonable explanation for having that."

I squinted at the plastic bag, which the chief dangled from her fingers. What reason could Barbara Lou have for carrying around Nick's hair? Some sick souvenir of her deadly deed?

Vaughn placed a hand on his sister's shoulder. "Barbie, maybe you should go with the chief. Clear everything up. I'll cancel the crew for today."

Barbara Lou's nostrils flared. "Whose side are you on?"

"Yours, of course."

"Did you do this to me? To protect your pathetic little wife?"

Vaughn jumped back. "My wife? I don't know what you're implying, but Ramona didn't—"

"Didn't love Nick?" Barbara Lou's accusation made her brother wince. "Spare me the faux outrage. We *both* know what she did for him."

Monday took a step forward. "Miz Sinclair, this doesn't need to get ugly."

Barbara Lou spun around and peered at all of us. I pulled Celeste closer, more for my safety than her comfort.

"Who brought the police here?" Barbara Lou's eyes settled on Celeste, whose body tensed. "You couldn't stand it, could you? Bad enough you took Pablo from me, but you had to do the same thing to Nick."

Celeste stepped out of our embrace and held her arms out defensively. "That's all in the past. We buried those skeletons long ago."

Tears welled in Barbara Lou's eyes. "I didn't."

Celeste dropped her arms and took another step toward her accuser. "Pablo was his own man. He did what we wanted. You never accepted that."

"Accept the things I cannot change?" Barbara Lou mocked. "Spare me your junkie platitudes."

Celeste's shoulders slumped, and she returned to Levi and me.

"Miz Sinclair, if you'll follow Officer Perkins, he'll escort—"

"What are you grinning at?" Barbara Lou spat in Trevor's direction.

Trevor froze at attention.

"Did you know that hair was in my bag? Did someone put you up to this?" When Trevor didn't answer, Barbara Lou stomped her foot. "Answer me, you Howdy Doody–looking errand boy."

"Miz Sinclair." Monday raised her hand, and the room went silent. "I'll grant you the courtesy of no handcuffs, but I reserve judgment on a muzzle."

"Someone in this room knows something." Barbara Lou glared at us as she moved toward the door. "Believe me. I'll find the rat." She exited the studio, with Officers Perkins and Whales stumbling to keep up.

Monday and I locked eyes, and she nodded.

"What's that about?" Levi whispered into my ear.

"What's what about?"

"Chief Malone just communicated something to you. I'm an expert in micro expressions."

"Really?" My lip curled. "What am I communicating now?"

"That's more of a macro expression."

"If this was a setup, I pity the poor soul who did it." Celeste's soft voice defused Levi's agitation. "You only have one opportunity to kill the queen."

"I won't get course credit for this if we don't shoot something," an intern groaned.

"It's time for the new coronation," Vaughn said. "Celeste, come retake your throne."

Celeste blinked. "Me?"

"You've done this before. You know the steps and how to move for the camera. I need to shoot something."

Celeste looked down at herself. "But I can't look like this. Give me a minute to change."

"I'll help how I can," Ramona said. "Most of what we have is sized for Barbie. I'll go see what we can piece together."

"Wait! She can wear some of my things!" Marisol, the opportunist, chased Ramona.

I put my hand on Celeste's shoulder. "You don't have to do this. Nick was probably murdered over this. Who cares about budgets, about internship course credits? You don't owe these people anything."

Celeste held her hands out. "It's showbiz, kid."

"No. It's aerobics."

Smiling, she asked, "Do you know the last time I starred in one of these? You were probably in middle school. Yes, this is all looney, but I'm not doing this for Vaughn or whiny interns." She grabbed my shoulder and whispered, "I've never starred in one of these sober. I want to prove I can do this. To myself. You can understand that."

I nodded.

She motioned to the set. "Will you stay? Back me up?"

I swallowed. "I'll yelp and squeal so loudly that you'll think I'm sprinting through the backwoods of Georgia."

Celeste lightly tapped my chin with her fist. "Thanks, kiddo. Save me a seat." She jogged away to change.

"Tanaka-san, what's up?" Levi placed both fists on his spandexed hips.

"She's determined to go on. She'll replace Barbara Lou."

"Naturally, that's showbiz. But that's not what I mean. These side conversations with Celeste, with the chief… What aren't you telling me?"

"I ran into Celeste last night. She mentioned something that made me think Barbara Lou knows more about Nick's murder than she's saying."

"You *ran* into her? Where were you last night?" Levi stepped back. "You interviewed a suspect without me?"

"Stop talking like that. She's not a sus—" I checked for eavesdroppers. "At an NA meeting."

"Narcotics Anonymous?" Levi's eyes widened.

"Shh. It won't be anonymous if you don't lower your voice."

"Sorry. What were you doing at a…? Did you…? Are you okay?"

"I'm fine. Mostly. I don't know."

"So, Celeste gave you some information, and you told Chief Malone instead of me?" Levi's face dropped, his voice almost a whisper.

"Our goal was to help Trevor. To clear his name?" I attempted a chuckle that sounded more like a throat clearing. "Well, mission accomplished, right? Right, Levi?"

"Mission accomplished. Were you ever going to tell me?"

"It was an NA meeting. I didn't want to expose Celeste by telling you what I learned. You don't understand the—"

"Direct me to my mark, Vaughn." Celeste jogged to the center of the set, bejeweled with a royal-blue sweatband and coordinating wrist and leg warmers. An eager-looking Marisol followed.

"Now you look like a star," Vaughn said. "You know your mark, doll. Hasn't been that long."

"Long enough." Celeste studied the ground as she moved her feet into place. "Can I have a rehearsal?"

"Anything you want. Now, the intern has the cue cards ready, but improvise however you want. I wrote those words for Barbie, so do what's comfortable for you. All right, people, quiet for a rehearsal." Vaughn held up three fingers. "And three, two…"

"Uh, hey, y'all. I'm… I mean, are you ready—"

"Let's stop a minute," Vaughn said. "Shake off those nerves, doll."

Celeste shook her hands. "Sorry. It's hot under these lights."

"Feels good to be out of the background," Vaughn said. "You've got this. Okay, people, one more time. Celeste, it's your show now." He held up three fingers for a countdown. "Three…"

"Vaughn, this doesn't feel right." Celeste staggered forward but quickly regained her balance. "I mean, I don't feel right."

"Focus on the camera." Vaughn's voice had a soothing quality. "Make that connection. Pretend no one else is here. And three, two…"

Celeste stood still.

"Doll?"

"Something's wrong," I said to Levi. "Celeste?"

"Sho, I feel dizzy. I feel sick—"

"You okay, doll?"

"Can we get some water?" I asked. "Here, you need to sit—"

In what felt like déjà vu, Celeste dropped to the floor.

Chapter 12

"OPEN YOUR EYES, TANAKA-SAN. Deep breath."

I'd done it again. I'd failed her.

"One. Two. Three. Breathe."

Failure. Loser. You did it again!

"Open your eyes."

I gasped from trying to breathe through my nose and mouth. Levi's face appeared above me, and he lightly pressed my shoulders to keep me stable. I turned my head to cough, realizing I was lying on a bench.

"The police had barely made it back to the station with

Barbara Lou when I called them," Levi said when I'd recovered. "We can wait here until someone takes our statements."

I recognized the grid of ceiling panels and overhead lights of the men's locker room. I didn't remember fainting, but watching Celeste collapse replayed in my mind. My face burned at the realization that I'd once again made a spectacle of myself. *Why can't I be stronger? What's wrong with me?*

"I overheard the chief," Levi said. "She wants to close the Lone Star and call in the county health department. Vaughn went bananas. A weird occasion to show everyone an actual personality."

"His sister was just taken in for questioning. I imagine he's upset."

"He didn't go bananas over Barbara Lou." Levi chuckled. "He doesn't want to disassemble and haul away all his video-editing equipment. Said it was an inconvenience."

"The county health department?" I repeated, trying and failing to keep up with the conversation. "Why would they inspect the Lone Star?"

"There's been a second suspicious death," Levi replied in a low voice.

"Death. So she's gone?" My lungs burned when I sucked in too much air, so I released it through ragged sobs. "Celeste?"

Levi shuffled his tennis shoes and made a noncommittal sound. He pushed a water bottle dripping with condensation into my open palm and closed my fingers around it. "If we're both going to sit around and ugly cry, we need to stay hydrated."

"Why her?" My voice sounded raspy and like it had come from someone else. I pulled myself up and twisted off the cap, then stared at it for a moment, replaying my poisoned-water theory. Taking a long drink, I realized I didn't really care anymore.

"Tanaka-san, I don't think Celeste was the target."

I shook my head, which caused nausea instead of clarity. "What do you mean?"

"How would the killer know the police would come for Barbara Lou? Or that Celeste would take Barbara Lou's spot in the video? Unless…" Levi tapped his chin. "Maybe Celeste called the cops. She assumed Vaughn would pick her to replace his sister. Of course, she didn't know she'd die over this."

A knot formed in my stomach. Levi's theory was logical, except my call the previous night was what had brought Chief Malone to the Lone Star this morning. Of course, Celeste could have set me up, dropping information about Nick's relationship with Barbara Lou to push me toward telling the chief. Somehow, the patsy theory felt more comfortable than the theory that Barbara Lou was the intended victim. That would make me responsible for Celeste's death.

"I'm sorry you're upset with me." I took another drink and shut my eyes.

"Sounds like a non-apology apology." Levi studied the invisible dirt under his fingernails.

"It's an explanation for why the police wanted to reinterview Barbara Lou. Last night, during her share, Celeste referenced fentanyl. How dangerous it is. How easy it is to obtain. Then Monday mentioned it—"

"The chief was at NA too?"

"That's a story for another day." I clamped my eyes tighter to trap any remaining focus. "Celeste also mentioned that Barbara Lou knew about Nick's smoking and that he wore nicotine patches during their fitness shoots, and it vexed her."

"Okay…" Levi's voice had an undercurrent of annoyance.

"Fentanyl and nicotine patches. The two gelled in my brain. That's why I phoned the chief. Nick put on a patch right before he collapsed. You can get liquid fentanyl. So perhaps…"

"Barbara Lou poisoned Nick's nicotine patch to teach him a lesson and keep her fitness brand shiny?"

Hearing it out loud made me cringe. "It's a stretch, but then there's the bag of hair in Barbara Lou's duffel. What's that about?"

Levi sat next to me on the bench. "Celeste collapsed just like Nick. Was she a smoker too?" He gasped. "Or was fentanyl her drug of choice—"

"Celeste was in recovery. Recovery was her choice." My snappish response ignited another coughing fit. Unfortunately, Levi had made another logical point. I wished he would stop. If Nick and Celeste had died from fentanyl, Celeste must have absorbed the poison somehow. *If she didn't ingest it, then…* "The sweatband!"

"The sweatband?"

"Celeste's sweatband. In her signature royal blue. That's how she absorbed the poison."

"Ramona got that from the storeroom. You're saying Celeste *was* the target?"

"I don't know what I'm saying." Waving my hand almost made me fall off the bench. "Except that fentanyl can be fatal to the touch. Monday! Levi, you must tell the chief—"

"The officers are wearing face masks and gloves. Sounds like Chief Malone bought into your theory. Kudos." Levi spoke with a clenched jaw, hurling every word like rapid gunfire.

I started to relitigate my case for concealing information gathered at NA when another knot formed. "What about Lulah? What's going to happen to Celeste's dog?"

She must have wondered, too, because the monkey-faced dog trotted through a back door, which was propped open with a bench. She sat at Levi's feet but blinked at me.

"Where'd she come from?" I asked.

"Door has a busted lock." Levi reached down to scratch her

ears. "I let Lulah out to make a nature call. She's bunking with me tonight."

I stared at the open back door, which I'd never noticed before, then turned to the locker row behind me. Nick had probably come in there to get his final nicotine patch. The killer could have slipped in from the outside, then out again unnoticed. I would have to consider that possibility after Officer Perkins finished taking our statements.

Perkins listened dutifully to us, displaying zero body language and offering no verbal cues that signaled his thoughts on anything. After my previous interactions with Perkins, it felt natural to converse with a human statue.

Monday arrived at some point to shoot me pitiful glances that only made my face burn. She also confirmed Nick had died from fentanyl poisoning. I'd been right. But that didn't feel so great.

"Thanks again for the tip, Tanaka," Monday said.

I mumbled and dared not look at Levi.

"Because of what you told me, my guys were prepared to safely handle Miz Gravell and her… effects."

"Test Celeste's sweatband for fentanyl." I bowed my head. "That's how it got into her system."

Officer Perkins drove me to the Cherry Blossom in his patrol car. Riding in his air-conditioned back seat like a criminal was preferable to driving a Segway through the Texas heat in a Hello Kitty helmet. I looked out the back window, noting Levi wasn't following us. The previous night, on the church steps, I'd debated whether I should call Levi or Monday first. I ended up not calling Levi at all. I'd made the right decision. Levi would see that, too—eventually.

Still wearing Ojii-chan's tracksuit, I crawled into my bed, pulled the quilt over my head, and tried to ignore the mind replay of Celeste dying.

NEWS OF CELESTE'S DEATH went viral, thanks to an internet video spotlighting Barbara Lou's verbal assault at the previous day's shoot. Someone posted the video anonymously with the title "Granny Gone Wild." It had also been scored with an upbeat song that reminded me of those slapstick silent films.

"It's rewinding. What's happening?" I sat upright in bed, cushioned by some pillows, watching the video on Levi's phone.

"It's just the editing." He sat next to me, chewing his breakfast sandwich, which I had a sneaking suspicion was mine. "See? Barbara Lou lunges at Celeste, the video rewinds, then Barbara Lou sounds like a chipmunk… then she lunges in slow motion."

"Tasteful."

The sound effect of a meowing cat blasted from the phone.

Levi batted at my shoulder like it was a ball of yarn. "That's my favorite part."

Setting the phone on the nightstand, I asked, "Why would Vaughn take this video? This is his sister. That can't be good for business."

"I don't think it was Vaughn." Levi wiped his fingers on a napkin. "My money is on one of those unpaid interns. I don't care what you say—no one enjoys getting paid with 'experience.'"

"It's terrible camera work, whoever took it. We see more of Barbara Lou's sequined head than anything else." I ticked names off on my fingers. "We're both in the video, so we didn't film it. Trevor and Celeste are there too." I focused on my four extended fingers. "What about Ramona?"

"She brought Barbara Lou the sweatband, but I don't remember seeing her during the confrontation."

"Possibly an important detail," I said. "Ramona presumably also gave Celeste her sweatband. And both Vaughn and Marisol were behind the camera. I think."

"Let's go talk to Vaughn. Even if he didn't post the video, he knows who did."

I groaned and sank back into my pillows. "Can't we let the police handle this?"

"What an illogical thing to say." Levi stood and set his plate on the floor. "The police are focused on the friction between Barbara Lou and Nick. Fine, but the entire Sinclair family has issues. Nick was horning in on that business. Maybe someone wanted to stop that."

"Agreed. And Celeste was also part of that family at one point."

"I still can't picture Celeste marrying Vaughn." Levi raised a finger. "Don't think I've forgotten about how you gained that information through your rogue investigating. We'll revisit that conversation later."

"Can't wait." I slid a little farther under the covers.

"Since I'm in a forgiving mood, I'll make you a deal. You go with me to see Vaughn, and I'll go with you to that hippy-dippy herbal store for those supplements. What's the name of those drops? Gecko bologna?"

"Ginkgo biloba." I groaned. "We shouldn't have to negotiate your health. Especially since our last bargain of training for a triathlon went so poorly."

Levi nodded. "Yeah, you still follow me right into my shenanigans."

I lifted the covers over my head to create a sound barrier. "Stupid bucket list."

Chapter 13

According to the sign on the door, the Lone Star was closed until further notice. But Levi had remembered the "loose" door that led from the back alley into the men's locker room. Sure enough, that door was still open, allowing us a somewhat ethical way of getting inside.

Levi knocked on Vaughn's open office door. "It's like a casino in here."

Vaughn faced his computer screen, consumed by a thick cloud of smoke. "We're closed today, guys. How did you even…?" He turned, and his gaze traveled to Levi's phone, which was playing the video of Barbara Lou's attacks. Vaughn stubbed out his cigarette and returned to his online poker game. "I guess everyone's seen it by now."

"We were just wondering how the footage you shot got anonymously posted on the internet."

"Son of a—" Vaughn slammed the computer mouse on his desk and muttered something at the monitor. He flashed an annoyed look at Levi's outstretched phone. "Are you questioning my professionalism? Our camera work is better than that. None of my crew shot that."

Levi raised the phone closer to his face. "He's right, Tanaka-san." He angled the phone toward me and pointed. "There's Vaughn's elbow."

"Notice what the camera is focused on," Vaughn said. "It's not my sister."

"It's her head." I grabbed Levi's phone and replayed the video. "Her sweatband, anyway. Wait." I paused and zoomed in on the sweatband, which was embroidered with Marisol's toucan logo. "Of course. Her phone is glued to her hand." Though I seemed to remember Celeste took Marisol's phone, the one with the videos of Nick's final moments.

Vaughn cleaned his glasses with his T-shirt. "Probably trying to create buzz for her athletic wear. Another one of Marisol's endless entrepreneurial endeavors."

"But why?" I asked. "So Barbara Lou would be wearing it when the police arrived?"

Did Marisol have her phone ready because she knew about the police? Was she trying to set up Barbara Lou, diverting suspicion from herself? Or was Marisol capitalizing on a possible internet "viral" moment that would promote her brand?

"We've got boxes of her stuff stacked in the storeroom," Vaughn said. "She wanted us to sell it here. The quality isn't terrible, but we're not interested in doing business with Marisol."

"Did it surprise you she was consulting for Barbara Lou?" I asked.

"Barbie stopped asking me for business advice years ago."

I jutted my chin at the online poker game Vaughn had been playing. "Because you're bad with money?"

"Tanaka-san…"

Vaughn swiveled his chair around to face me, but he kept the thin smile. "I'm blowing off a little steam. What happened yesterday jeopardizes this gym's future."

"How so? Were there plans to feature Celeste in future videos?" Levi asked.

"I mean Barbie being questioned by the police." Vaughn swiveled back to start a new poker game. "And on camera!" He banged the mouse on his desk again.

"Do you think your sister killed Nick?" I asked.

Vaughn clicked on the backs of a few virtual cards, revealing his poker hand. "It doesn't matter if Barbie killed him. People will think she did. It's all about perception." He sighed at his computer monitor and flicked it with his hand.

I bit my lip to control my annoyance with Vaughn's priorities. Having two murders in his gym seemed like more of a concern than public perception. On one hand, Nick's death—and an attempt on Barbara Lou's life—seemed to eliminate Vaughn as a suspect. Both seemed more valuable to him alive than dead. However, Vaughn would presumably benefit financially from his sister's death, and even a short-gain sales spike of Nick's videos might be enough of a motive to kill. *Unless…*

"Do you believe Barbara Lou was the intended victim yesterday?"

"Makes sense." Vaughn maneuvered his chair back around but remained fixed on his poker game. "The person who took out Nicky also wanted to take out Barbie."

"Why, though?" That part was still bothering me. Who benefited from eliminating Nick and Barbara Lou?

"Maybe to hurt me," Vaughn said quietly.

What a ridiculously self-centered answer. "Why would someone murder two people to hurt you?"

Vaughn tugged at the fabric of his chair's arms. "Barbie isn't as popular as she once was, even with Nick. Our production costs are high, and, well, it always seemed like the move to digital cameras and editing software cheapened the quality of the final product. Maybe I should have adapted quicker, because I tied most of my equity up in this money pit of a gym." He laughed. "I owe money to some people." He gazed longingly at his online poker game as if it were his financial lifeline. "I'm late on the payments, and the interest is adding up."

Marisol had indicated Vaughn was desperate for money, maybe desperate enough to consider selling the entire catalog of fitness content. Admittedly, I'd chalked those claims up as more Marisol bluster.

"These aren't bank loans, then?" Levi asked. "Are you suggesting bookies killed Nick and Celeste? Retaliation for late payments? How much do you owe?" Levi arched an eyebrow in disbelief.

Vaughn continued to stare at his computer screen.

Scratching my chin, I said, "We're assuming Barbara Lou was the intended victim, but perhaps Celeste was the target." I stomped my foot to jar Vaughn out of his poker haze. "Who had a motive for killing Celeste?"

I replayed the sequence of the previous day's events. Ramona could easily have applied fentanyl to the sweatband Celeste wore.

How would Ramona know Celeste would replace Barbara Lou? And why would Ramona kill Celeste? I didn't even recall observing the two interact. Vaughn had said the sweatbands were in the storeroom, so conceivably, anyone could access them. But when? And how would the killer know Celeste, not Barbara

Lou, would be the one to wear the poisoned fabric? I was the only person who knew the police might arrive the previous day.

"Celeste was the best," Vaughn said in response to my question. He pushed up his glasses and grappled for the pack of cigarettes. "Who would want her dead?"

"She shared a connection with Nick," I said. "As she was his sponsor, Nick confided in her. Shared secrets other people might want to keep hidden."

Vaughn balanced an unlit cigarette with his fingers. "Anyone who knew Celeste knew her integrity. She wasn't like the other town biddies." He glared up at me and Levi. "Whatever Nick told her, she took to the grave."

I breathed deeply to calm my anxiety and tried another tactic. "Celeste told me about her early career in aerobics. About how you helped her and how Barbara Lou sabotaged her."

Vaughn gave a bitter laugh. "Unless Barbara Lou is the street name for some drug, my sister played no role in Celeste's downfall. She sabotaged herself. Barbie insisted on keeping her employed. She thought the distraction of work might clean Celeste up and establish some goals other than staying high twenty-four, seven."

Celeste had described a similar response to Barbara Lou helping Nick. Was the story about Barbara Lou poisoning Celeste even true?

The cigarette rolled off Vaughn's desk when he wiped his eyes. "Celeste was always sharp, but some of her fitness ideas were a little looney. Maybe because of the drugs. She wanted a career in facial aerobics."

"That's a thing?" Levi asked.

"Another decades-old fad," Vaughn said. "Some quack of a doctor told Celeste that stretching the facial muscles stimulated the blood flow, made your skin glow, and reduced the *'gobble-gobble'* look." He fluttered his fingers underneath his neck to demonstrate. "This was the same quack who prescribed her loads of weight loss drugs too. Made her even more looney. She'd sit and focus on a task for hours before collapsing from exhaustion." He inhaled raggedly. "Those were some crazy times."

"The video you wanted to produce with Barbara Lou and Celeste, the Gal Pals fitness video? That was your attempt to focus Celeste on a more serious career?"

"What video?" Levi asked me.

Vaughn nodded. "And Celeste got *sick*."

"*Sick*?" I echoed. "Barbara Lou upped her laxatives."

Levi blinked at me. "What are you talking about? When did you learn all this?"

"I don't know what happened there." Vaughn finger-parted his thinning hair. "I was trying to manage my temperamental wife, who went from zero to sixty in a split second." He snapped for emphasis. "Honestly, I barely remember that version of Celeste anymore. She turned her life around after the accident."

I pressed my lips together, considering my next question. "Could Celeste's death be connected to the death of her first husband? Pablo Alvarado? He was a good friend of yours, correct?"

Levi frowned. "Her *first* husband? I thought you said…? Who is Pablo Alvarado?"

Vaughn jerked his head up in surprise. "You're asking me about things I haven't thought about in years."

"But Barbara Lou's thought about it. She mentioned Pablo to Celeste yesterday, right before she left with the police."

A crash from behind us startled me. I turned around to an empty hallway and a pungent whiff of rose water.

"Pablo died almost thirty years ago," Vaughn said. "There's no connection between him and what happened to Celeste."

I turned back to face him, chewing the inside of my cheek. "Did Pablo and Barbara Lou have a child?"

Vaughn grabbed the unlit cigarette and stubbed it into his

desk. "Family business stays in the family." He swiveled his chair around and resumed his game of poker.

"WAIT, TANAKA-SAN. Who's Pablo Alvarado?"

I turned to answer him but saw Ramona emerging from behind the trio of stair-climbers.

"Celeste was the love of his life," she said, surprising Levi, who hadn't noticed her. "Even my family money couldn't compete with Vaughn's first love." She scoffed. "Some trophy wife I am."

"I'm sorry, Ramona," Levi said. "I shouldn't be blurting those things here."

"It's been a stressful time." She patted his hands and nodded. "We've lost two members of our family. They're irreplaceable."

"How was your relationship with Celeste?" I asked. "I never saw you two interact."

Ramona's eyes went blank, but her head kept bobbing. "You know she was Vaughn's first wife. And obviously, you know she was also my brother's first wife." Her head dropped. "His only wife."

"So there was friction between you two?" I asked.

Levi shot me an annoyed look. "Maybe we can chat some other time."

Ramona lifted her head. "I knew what I was getting into when I married a Sinclair. Celeste and I were… cordial. No *friction*. And I'm sure Vaughn was already clear about our family business staying in the family." She shot me a grin. "And as much as we get a kick out of y'all, you're not family."

"Right, and family protects family. Blood is thicker than water, and all that jazz." I included jazz hands for effect.

"Tanaka-san, what's wrong? You never use choreography."

Ramona wagged a finger at me. "You're teasing me, Mr. Tanaka, but yes, all that's true."

I raised my eyebrows. "Is that why you poisoned Barbara Lou?"

Ramona froze.

"Tanaka-san, what are you talking about?"

"I didn't poison my sister-in-law. She was poisoning herself with those laxatives. I might have just doubled the dose. By accident." She giggled.

"What laxatives?" Levi asked.

I waved him away. "I'll tell you later."

"Tell me now—"

"I guess it's an open secret," I continued. "Nick goaded you about his smoothie when we first met, and Barbara Lou joked about it as well."

"She did the same thing to Celeste years ago." Ramona tossed her head. "What's good for the goose."

"But you weren't acting on Celeste's behalf." I crossed my arms and studied her. "You loved your brother."

Ramona's back straightened, and she crossed her arms to mirror me. "Pablo was an exceptional human being."

"And opioids tragically cut his life short," I said. "My sister and I aren't close. We used to be, but... Well, even now, I can't imagine my life without her in it."

Ramona widened her eyes, likely to stop the tears.

"Who do you blame when something like that happens?" I asked.

Levi placed a hand on my shoulder. "I think we'd better—"

"The town gossip mill claims your brother was a junkie," I continued. "That he got hooked on opioids."

"Pablo was no *junkie*." Ramona's bottom lip quivered. "He was a kind, loyal, loving man. She knew that, too, and she used it to destroy him."

"Who did?" I prompted. "Barbara Lou?"

"He died before the world got to see the truly great man he would've become. She took that away from me, from my family. She drove Pablo to the edge with her lies, demands, and extortion."

"So poisoning Barbara Lou wasn't to help Nick either? Sure, he benefited from it, but you were using him too. You knew he'd rise to the occasion and that his ego was healthy enough that he'd use the opportunity to advance himself. And he did. He hired Marisol, who prodded him to quit the Lone Star. But more important, he pulled away from Barbara Lou. That's what you wanted."

Ramona released a shaky breath. "Nick went ballistic when I told him what I'd done. Almost punched a hole in the wall above me." She hugged herself. "But yes, once he calmed down, he certainly didn't seem to mind what happened."

I tapped my chin. "Knowing Nick, I'm sure he probably used the situation to his advantage."

"He stopped respecting me and started undermining me. His smoking cost the gym money, but he didn't care."

"Even you couldn't anticipate the size of Nick's ego. Leading me to your brother's death and your poisoning of Barbara Lou."

Ramona shook her head. "There's no connection between those events."

I smirked. "You don't see the correlation between your brother's drug overdose and Nick's nearly identical cause of death?"

"Let's get some air, Tanaka-san."

Ramona revealed a set of keys to unlock the front door. "Listen to your friend. Get out."

"You recreated Barbara Lou's alleged poisoning of Celeste. Why wouldn't you also recreate the circumstances that killed your brother? It's genius, actually." I shrugged off Levi's grip. "But even killing Nick didn't curb your appetite for revenge."

"Get out. Get out, please." Ramona's hands shook at she struggled to unlock the door.

"You couldn't bear to see Barbara Lou retake the spotlight." I raised a fist to my mouth. "It must have been torture, watching her strut around in all those sequins, giving Vaughn direction, and allowing Marisol to degrade you the way she did. You needed to finish what you started."

"Tanaka-san. Outside. Air." Levi again grabbed my shoulder, that time pulling me back.

I charged at Ramona, my shoes squeaking against the rubber floors. "You almost got it too." Ramona wrapped her arms around her waist, flinching at each word I hurled. "Celeste wasn't your intended target, but you're not sad she's gone either."

Purple-faced, Ramona opened her mouth and unleashed an explosive scream. "Get out!" She doubled over, gagging from the vocal strain. "Get out now!" She punctuated her screaming with gasps and dry heaves.

"You dressed Celeste, giving her that poisoned sweatband."

"Poisoned?" Ramona gulped for air. "That sweatband was already in the locker room when we arrived. Marisol must have—"

Levi grabbed me by both shoulders and shoved me out the door. It slammed behind us, and he pushed a hand against my back to propel me forward.

"Don't come back here. Ever!" I could still hear Ramona's raspy coughs through the door.

Chapter 14

"WHAT WAS THAT?" Levi asked.

I flapped my arms to pull out of Levi's grip. When he let go, I stumbled forward into the gym's parking lot.

"Thanks for the backup." I wiped the sweat from my upper lip. "We could have gotten a full confession from Ramona if you hadn't grabbed me."

"I'm surprised your head didn't spin around, and you spider-walked out here. What has gotten into you?"

"Ugh, spare me the rerun of another lecture. Are you implying I'm *on* something again?"

"What? No! I've just never seen you that confrontational." Levi stepped back slightly.

I curled my lip. "Never had a reason to be. Until now."

Levi kicked at the gravel. "Celeste's death has affected you. Are you even aware of that enough to process it?"

"I'm angry."

"Understood. But you can't just accuse people of murder like that. These are real people, real families. Isn't that what you're always telling me?"

I shook my head. "Uh, I'm sorry. Did we just meander into some alternate universe where you spout sensible things?"

"I'm always sensible. You're just too busy snarking and making up words like *meander.*" Levi held out his hands and took a breath. "I felt a little ambushed in there. I'm confused about Pablo Alvarado… and a secret love child? Barbara Lou's history of poisoning? And Ramona used these poisoning methods against her? Where did all these theories come from?"

"I told you! From Celeste. I also told you why I kept it private."

Levi waved a hand in the air. "It's not private when you hurl it at suspects during interrogations."

"Wow." I rolled my eyes. "Two people are dead. Murdered. And I've got a solid theory about who did it. Meanwhile, you've got your *Tween of the Crime* boxers in a bunch because I didn't share a few details."

"I respect your privacy, Tanaka-san, and why you didn't want to tell me you went to a meeting. But what Celeste told you wasn't related to your recovery or hers. I thought we were in this together." He folded his arms and turned away. "For the record, *Tween of the Crime* boxers don't exist. There was a limited run of bikini briefs, though. Now I've spoiled your birthday surprise."

Adjusting the lapels of my blazer, I said, "This is ridiculous."

"Agreed. Let's go back to the café, have our second breakfast, and regroup."

"No. No more. You know, from the moment we met, you've ripped through my life like a tornado. Within the first thirty-six hours of meeting you, I got beat up, accused of murder, and almost killed. Thinking about it still gives me whiplash."

"You also confessed that the thrill of adventure made you reevaluate your priorities. It's not like you were living your best life before me. And don't forget—you shared things with me you still won't tell Jenny."

I stepped toward him. "Is that a threat?"

"Of course not." Levi's eyes drooped, and his shoulders sagged. "But you're hiding out here in Bluebonnet Hills, whether you want to admit it or not. Your jokes about overeating and sneaking extra glasses of wine? Those are all symptoms of a root cause. You're not dealing with that reality."

"Well, you're certainly the in-house expert on reality." I gave Levi a slow clap for his diagnosis. "Helping Trevor, stimulating your brain… Those aren't the reasons you're investigating these murders. You want publicity. You want to reboot your career and perhaps even reboot your show. Just like Trevor so innocently suggested."

"If that's what you think, maybe we're not friends."

"Yeah, these six weeks have formed an indestructible bond." I punched my open palm. "I don't need your help. I'm not your sidekick, and I'm definitely not one of your strays."

"One of my what?"

"I'm not a falsely accused orphan like Trevor. Or a homeless puppy like Lulah. You're a magnet for broken things. You draw energy from other people's misery."

Levi stared blankly. Finally, he turned toward his Segway. "Enjoy the solo investigating. You'll understand if I don't feel like shopping for dinkus bovine today."

"Ginkgo biloba!" I shouted as Levi drove out of the parking lot. "It's a powerful antioxidant that fights inflammation!"

I ran after him, but he'd turned onto Mockingbird Lane. "It also improves brain function and can reduce depression and anxiety!"

A hot breeze whipped my hair as I spun back around. I kicked the asphalt, skidded across some gravel, and flopped onto my tailbone. Stunned, I blinked up at the sun before staggering up and limping toward my Segway.

Not my classiest exit, but I got the last word.

I BOUNDED UP THE STAIRS to my bedroom, not bothering to acknowledge anyone at the Cherry Blossom Café.

Flinging open my closet doors, I planned a full-on dramatic tossing of clothes into my suitcase. But the closet was mostly empty because I'd been living out of my suitcase since I arrived in Bluebonnet Hills with only about a week's worth of clothes. My e-reader lay on the nightstand, though, so I chucked that into my suitcase for the desired effect.

Jenny appeared in the doorway, carrying a tray with two blue vintage porcelain cups and saucers.

"Thanks, but I'm not in the mood for tea." I swatted the air.

Jenny set the tray down on my bed. "Good, because it's sake."

"*That*, I'm in the mood for." I lifted a cup and held it with both hands. Warming the sake had intensified its woody scent. "It's barely the afternoon. Is the power of yes driving you to drink?"

"Something like that." Jenny clinked her cup against mine and took a sip. "I see you're packing. Were you going to let me know?"

I drank some sake, shivering from the fermented alcohol. "I don't know what I'm doing. Just don't want to be here."

"What's wrong with here?"

"Not for me. Too much drama, too many people butting into your life, probing you for information."

"You mean the whole community thing? Yeah, it stinks to be surrounded by people who look out for you. I don't know how you stand it."

"Most of these people need to get their own lives." I closed my suitcase as the reality of having nowhere to go settled in. "I see how someone like you could thrive here, but we're not the same."

Jenny toasted me with her cup. "I'll drink to that."

"What's that supposed to mean?"

"I'm agreeing with you." She took a long drink. "I love it here. This town has allowed me to be my own person, open my café, try my recipes, and bring a little of my culture here. You're more, eh, closed-minded and crusty."

I spun around, almost spilling my drink. "I'm not Nanny Poppycock Two-Point-Oh. I'm nobody's scone."

Jenny blinked. "I won't even pretend to understand that." She scrunched her nose. "You and Levi got into a fight, didn't you?"

"Why would you ask that?"

"Because he just left. He picked up his second breakfast and his first lunch to go." She giggled. "It was quite a sight, watching him balance all those takeout boxes. Luckily, he finished half his meal before he got to his Segway."

I shook my head. "We fought. As much as you can fight with someone whose only references are ninety-seven episodes of a canceled tween-detective TV series."

Jenny raised a finger in protest. "Don't forget the two-part Arbor Day special."

I raised my arms. "Who could forget Arbor Day?"

"What did you fight about?"

"I learned some information that might reveal who murdered Nick and Celeste. Levi was mad I didn't share it with him first."

"How did you get this information? Where was he?"

I held my breath. It wasn't an appropriate time to tell Jenny I'd attended a Narcotics Anonymous meeting. Her body stiffened, like she was waiting for me to confess everything. Instead, I said, "That's… uh… complicated."

Her upper body crumpled. "Why wouldn't you share with Levi? Aren't you both trying to help Trevor? Plus, he's your friend."

"I barely know him."

"Hmm. Crusty *and* obtuse." Jenny set her drink on the nightstand to cross her arms. "You know, you two have more in common than you care to admit. Bluebonnet Hills is new to Levi too. And he wants to do a good job as mayor. The position weighs on him. I see it in his face. He relies on you. Trusts you. I see that too."

"I don't know how to be friends with someone that unpredictable. That aimless. He lives in a TV show, and I live in the real world."

Jenny blew a raspberry. "You're living out of a suitcase, sleeping in your little sister's spare bedroom, in a town you've never visited. Not exactly the *real world.*"

Point to Jenny. I craned my neck and crouched under the bed. "Any more of those pore strips lying around? I have the sudden urge to rip one off your nose." I grinned.

Jenny flopped on the foot of the bed, patting the space beside her. I sat down next to her.

"You know, Sho-chan, I used to think we drifted apart because I did something wrong. But you push away anyone who wants to know you better. Why is that? What are you afraid of?"

"With you, I always think of myself as your big brother. I'm the person who's supposed to be a role model. Instead, as you so eloquently stated, I'm squatting in your spare bedroom."

"Are we ever going to talk about this?"

"Talk about what?"

"About what's going on. Why you're here, in Bluebonnet Hills. Growing up, you never had these crippling panic attacks. Now they seem like a regular thing, and you're trying to hide them. Something happened in Seattle that you don't want to tell me." She elbowed me before I could protest. "And Ma notices, too, so don't say I'm imagining it."

I tugged at my hair. "There are some things I don't want to talk about. Yet. Besides, I'm enjoying my visit with you."

"About that." Jenny bounced her legs against the bed. "Any idea how much longer you'll be *visiting*?"

I wiped my clammy palms on the quilt. "Do you want me to leave?"

"You know I love that you're here, Sho-chan. Love that we're reconnecting." She inhaled deeply before facing me. "But you can't mope around all day then gripe about moping around all day. Be a visitor. Call yourself whatever you want, but find a purpose while you're here. Join a book club. Get a part-time job. Do something."

"Perhaps solve crimes with a former-tween-detective -slash-current-town-mayor?"

"It's something. And something different. We all get into ruts, so take advantage of your time here. Harness your yes." She nuzzled her head against my shoulder. "Not like you have anywhere else to be."

I raised my shoulder to give her head a little bounce. "Brat."

"I'd better get back downstairs. Some of us have jobs." Jenny sprang to her feet with a giggle and grabbed her sake. "You should go out tonight."

"Alone?"

"Isn't that your preference?" She shrugged. "A new wine bar opened up, right off the square. Take a nap and maybe another shower, and go have a drink. Or seven."

That seemed reasonable. I could use a glass of wine—or seven. "Can I borrow your car?"

"To drink? At a bar? That's a two-minute walk away? I hardly think so." She glanced over her shoulder. "And don't bring anyone home with you."

So much for the power of yes.

Chapter 15

W HEN I PUSHED OPEN the door of Uncork'd, I was greeted by an array of overstuffed seating around round bistro-style tables.

I turned and stepped up into the second room, which housed an L-shaped bar. The lighting was dim, giving an appropriate ambiance for the wallowing I had planned. When I moved to a stool, I noticed Marisol in the corner across from me. She was tapping at her phone with one hand and clutching a wine stem with the other.

She looked up and blinked in recognition, then smirked and asked, "What's new, Pussycat?"

"No helmet tonight." I knocked on my head for emphasis. "I walked here all on my own."

"Such a strapping big man." Marisol rocked on her stool, cupping her half-empty wineglass. It clearly wasn't her first... or her second. "Where's your hottie friend?"

I glanced over my shoulder. "My hottie who?"

"You know, your catnipped crusader. Everyone's favorite washed-up tween. The mayor with those plump, kissable lips."

"Levi?" I chuckled at the description. "I always considered his lips more punchable."

"Aww, did you two have a little catfight?" She slumped forward, her elbows keeping her upright.

I slipped off my blazer and hung it on the back of my stool. "Something like that." I caught the bartender's attention and ordered a glass of the house pinot grigio.

"You know, you're not too bad-looking yourself."

Tapping my fingers against the bar top, I replied, "Thank you."

"Especially after a few glasses of these." Marisol hoisted her wineglass.

Uh... thanks?

When the bartender set down a paper napkin and my wineglass, I studied the glass, contemplating how drunk I needed to get. *Stinking* was the adjective that came to mind. I glanced across the bar at Marisol. The text-typing sound flew furiously from her phone. "You waiting for a date?"

Marisol looked up and cocked her head. "My party planner."

I shrugged and pulled the wineglass toward me. "Sorry. Just making conversation."

"Is it true what they say about Asians and alcohol?"

This should be good. "What do *they* say?"

"Don't get offended. I'm Latin," she offered as justification for whatever offensive thing she was about to blurt. "I just heard your cheeks get all red when you drink booze."

That actually had some truth to it. Some Asians, particularly East Asians, lacked an enzyme that broke down alcohol. Besides turning the face tomato red, the 'Asian Flush' increased heart rate and activated nausea. There were other increased risks of diseases and cancers, but I sensed my scientific explanation was not what Marisol wanted. Instead, I toasted her with my pinot and winked. "Stick around and find out."

She laughed lightly and somehow glided across to the next barstool in one fluid movement. She batted her eyelashes at the bartender and pushed her empty glass forward, signaling for another.

"How much longer are you in town?" I asked.

Marisol scoffed. "Leaving tomorrow. I can't stand this place. Surprised there's not a bar on every corner." She turned to the window behind her, searching for something.

"Did you make any progress negotiating with Vaughn for his fitness catalog?" I asked. "I suspect Barbara Lou's cache went up after you posted that video."

Marisol jerked her head back around. "You saw that, huh? Yeah, she trended a bit. Videos of crazy old people will do that."

"You told us Celeste took your phone."

"And she keeled over before I could get it back. Had to buy a replacement." She stared into her wineglass and seemed surprised when the bartender replaced it with a full one. "All that video I took of Nicky's final moments. Gone." She shrugged. "Lost my phone and some valuable content, and Nicky sacked me."

"Nick fired you? When?"

"Right before he dropped dead. He'd done it before, but it still ticked me off. I took a drive to Austin to check out the action. That's why no one could find me."

"Forgive me for prying, but why did he fire you?" I drank my pinot and let the flavors of lime, green apple, and honey linger on my tongue.

"Nicky had these holier-than-thou streaks. I'd skipped a few of those stupid meetings, and he got pissy." She glanced up at me. "I assume you know about all that, since you caught me outside the church."

I nodded. "You didn't want to attend NA?"

Marisol swirled her rosé around her glass. "Another one of Nicky's stupid conditions for signing an exclusive with me."

"But you weren't serious about recovery?"

"I was serious about closing the deal. Serious about making some dough-re-mi." She took a long drink. "And that word. *Recovery.* No need to recover from a little recreational blow."

Her admission got both the bartender and me to raise our eyebrows, but he pretended to focus on cleaning his glassware.

Marisol didn't appear to notice or care. "Nicky wanted Celeste to be my sponsor, but she had an angle too. Just like everyone else."

I set my glass down. "Angle? What do you mean?"

"She pitched it to me a few months ago. A beginner's approach to fitness. You know, simple moves, nothing too strenuous. Not really my brand, but she seemed like a decent teacher."

"She was." Celeste had volunteered a lot of information about herself, but her desire to work with Marisol wasn't one of them. "Did Nick share his secrets with you?" Celeste might not have been forthcoming, but a soused Marisol might. "Everyone alludes to this dark past of his."

"Dark." Marisol snorted. "I mean, yeah, he was an addict and a dealer. Big friggin' deal. His NA shares were as boring as everyone else's. He did a lot of desperate things for money and hurt loads of people along the way. Blah, blah, wah, wah. After a while, all those stories ran together. It was one big whine fest." She shook her empty glass at the bartender. "And not my preferred kind of wine fest."

"Hurt people? How do you mean?"

"It was Narcotics Anonymous not Narcotics Announcements."

Marisol flipped through her phone before craning her neck to look out the window. "Nicky was upset about some guy he killed."

The bartender had left to locate another bottle of rosé, so he missed that bombshell. "He *killed* someone?" I used the napkin to blot some of the wine I'd spit.

"Not literally, bozo. It was an unintentional overdose." Marisol rolled her eyes. "Nicky sold some drugs that were stronger than he thought." She waved her phone in the air. "Anyway, this guy OD'd. Some other people died, too, but Nicky always fixated on this one particular guy." She scoffed. "Said he was a family man who didn't deserve to die."

The bartender returned and presented her with another glass.

"A junkie is a junkie." Marisol winked at me. "Some of us just party more responsibly than others."

I was reminded of a line from Celeste's share: *I'd be okay if I learned to smoke meth socially—like a lady.* Marisol had placed herself in that category of the socially acceptable drug user.

"This man's death, is it what brought Nick to Bluebonnet Hills?" It occurred to me that both Nick and I had fled to the town to escape drug-related incidents. I pushed my wineglass away.

"I always assumed Nicky was running from the law," Marisol said. "He apparently looked pretty lame and poor when he got here, so I guess all the working out and capped teeth changed his appearance. Made him comfortable enough to be on camera." She shrugged. "Didn't stop Barbara Lou from ratting him out, though."

"Oh? She knew about Nick's past?"

"If you ask me, she's the one who killed him. Celeste too." She leaned in. "She called me one night and tried to use Nicky's past as leverage. As if."

"You mean Barbara Lou wanted you to dump Nick and sign her instead?"

"What an upgrade, right?" Marisol sipped her wine. "Yeah,

she told me Nicky was a fraud, and I'd be foolish to sign him. I told her I knew everything already and didn't care. Your past is just that. Past."

The wine had only intensified the swirling in my head. Barbara Lou had reemerged as a suspect, perhaps believing murdering both Nick and Celeste would allow her to break out from her current dynasty and establish a new one. Celeste was trying to rebuild her career with Marisol's help, possibly diminishing Barbara Lou's chances of a contract. Did that give her a motive to murder Nick, though?

Marisol's phone dinged, announcing a text message. So far, Marisol was full of a lot of swagger, but I'd yet to hear about any of her grand ideas becoming realities. Still, murdering the same people you were trying to recruit seemed like bad business.

"Ugh, my party planner got spooked." Marisol glanced over her shoulder. "Must've thought you were with me." She wiggled off her stool and slunk toward me. "All this talk about Nicky and his entourage of Golden Girls is killing my buzz. I'm moving the party to my hotel room. Why don't you stop by later?"

I assumed my presence had interrupted a drug deal between Marisol and her *planner*. "I don't want to intrude on your *date*."

"You like labels, don't you?" She leaned over and whispered into my ear, "Does it make you feel more in control?" She turned to the side, supporting her weight by placing a hand on the bar. "Relax, Chairman Meow Meow. It's not a date. More like a business transaction." She removed her hand from the bar top, revealing a key to a hotel room. "I'm staying at the Bluebonnet Inn, Room 227."

My face heated but not from the wine. I glanced at the bartender, who waggled his eyebrows in a primal congratulatory response.

"I've got enough party favors for two," Marisol said before she stumbled out the door.

I drained my glass of pinot and stared at the room key. "Another glass, please," I said to the bartender.

Silently, he uncorked the bottle and poured. "A buddy of mine runs a ride-share business," he said. "You know, if you need a car for any reason."

My eyes drifted to the key as I slugged back the wine.

MY BODY SLUMPED FORWARD when the car stopped, then my head snapped back into the headrest. The three glasses of wine I'd drunk had made me sleepy, but Marisol's invitation excited me in a way I hadn't felt since arriving in Bluebonnet Hills.

Sure, she could be a murderer. But that somehow increased the thrill. That she had "party favors" was the actual draw.

Perhaps Marisol had a point—one could learn to party responsibly.

Besides, a little time with her wouldn't kill me. At best, it would clear my mind of the murders, erase the guilt over watching Nick and Celeste die and doing nothing to help them. And forget about my sister's supervision and Levi's ridiculousness.

"Have a good night, sir." The driver cleared the GPS information from his phone.

I'll stay fifteen minutes, I rationalized as I closed the car door behind me. *Thirty at the most.* Marisol probably partied a little harder than I was willing to, so perhaps I would just pop in, satisfy my curiosity, and pop back out. Yeah, I would stay forty-five minutes maximum.

After tripping over the parking lot's curb, I stumbled up to a stretch of lighted hotel room doors. I blinked to better focus on the numbers and followed the doors on my right, searching for Room 227.

I inhaled to calm my nerves before knocking softly. Though I had a key, I was still a gentleman, after all.

No one answered the door, and I heard no movement from the other side. I knocked again a little harder. "Marisol? It's Sho. Sho Tanaka."

Smooth, I thought. *You don't want to be confused with all the other Shos she slipped her hotel key to.*

I glanced at the parking lot behind me, which was filled with cars, but I didn't know what Marisol drove. Though I reached for my phone to call the driver back, I grabbed the hotel key instead.

Holding the key in my outstretched hand, I sucked in a breath. Technically, it wasn't breaking and entering. I had a key and an invitation. After I slipped the card into the slot, I waited for the red light to turn green. As I pushed the door open slowly, I noticed the TV was on, but the sound was muted. The lamps on both the side tables were also lit.

"Marisol. Uh, you left your key at the bar. I... I'm returning it."

Wow. The years I'd spent with my fiancée depleted any game I'd had with the opposite sex.

A sliver of light shone through the bathroom door. Perhaps Marisol was showering, but I couldn't hear any running water. I stood in the middle of the room, holding my breath and listening to the hum of the bathroom fan.

I knocked on the bathroom door. "Marisol?" Perhaps she was sick. She'd drunk at least a bottle of rosé.

When I pushed on the bathroom door, it hit something. I attempted to peer through the crack, but all I saw were the sterile white walls synonymous with hotel bathrooms.

I pushed the door a little harder, moving away whatever was blocking its path. As I scanned down the room, I noticed Marisol.

She was wedged between the corner and the commode. The heel of her shoe had been the object obstructing the door.

"Marisol! Marisol!"

I moved into the bathroom and crouched between her and the tub. When my hand brushed the back of her calf, it felt warm. I reached to check her pulse, noticing the hairbrush she'd been holding had rolled under the sink.

Adrenaline pulsed through me, causing my elbow to clip a trash can. Fumbling to keep the can upright, I noticed two crumpled patches at the bottom.

They had to be fentanyl patches. But did they belong to Marisol, or was she poisoned? And if she was poisoned, why aren't the patches still on her skin? I looked again at the hairbrush Marisol had likely been holding when she collapsed.

My legs throbbed as I pushed up from the floor and out of the bathroom. I dug for my phone, but a banging on the door caused me to drop it.

"Police. Open up, please."

I grabbed my phone and turned it over, confirming it hadn't called for help on its own.

The knocking continued, inducing enough sweat to detox me a second time. I glanced back at the bathroom and Marisol's shoeless foot.

If this wasn't a time to panic, when was?

Chapter 16

Though the interview room at the Bluebonnet Hills Police Department would never make the cover of an architectural magazine, it served its purpose. The locked room with no windows had medicinal white walls to elicit that ragged gasp of claustrophobia. Cold metal furniture scraped knee caps when banged into the table.

It didn't have the intended effect on me, though. I craved quiet, and the absence of sound suggested the walls had some soundproofing. The room was filled with soft light that hit me from all directions, not the shadowy darkness in the movies.

I looked around for the one-way mirror, disappointed there wasn't one.

A camera in the corner, just under the ceiling, captured my stoic silence. I considered offering a Levi Blue–style shimmy as consolation to whoever had to watch me.

"Thought you might need this."

I'd missed Monday's entrance. She set a paper cup of tea in front of me. "That tea bag was here when I got hired, so fair warning."

Glancing at the pathetic-looking cloudy water in front of me, then at the coffee mug that Monday held, I asked, "No tea for you, Chief?"

She settled in the chair across from me, a sheepish smile creeping across her face. "Not much of a tea drinker."

"Shocking." I raised my hands to my cheeks in faux surprise. Monday clearly hadn't enjoyed the bitterness of the green tea she'd drunk with me the other day. But it fulfilled her purpose of relating to me so that she could drag out information about Nick's death.

"Wine makes me you sassy. Haven't decided if I like it or not." She removed a pen from the spiral coil of her notepad. "I read the statement you gave Officer Perkins, but your story has some holes that need plugging. Let's start with why you were in Miz Montenegro's hotel room."

"Monte…" I shook my head, which induced a wave of nausea. "I… I didn't know Marisol's last name."

"Sassy and classy." Monday clicked her tongue and her pen. "You frequent strangers' hotel rooms often?"

"You're twisting my words."

"Untangle 'em for me."

"She'd left her room key at the bar. I was… returning it."

"A real live boy scout, eh?" She scribbled some notes and clicked her pen again. "To clarify, you used Miz Montenegro's key to get into her room so that you could return her key? That about right, Tanaka?"

"Yes. No. I mean, she was already in her room."

"Let's have another go-around then." She enunciated each word as she asked, "What were you doing there tonight?"

I swallowed and found my throat dry, so I lifted the cup of tea and sipped. It tasted like pond sludge, but it provided some moisture. "Is Marisol alive?"

"Telling Perkins about those trash-can patches saved her life. She OD'd, but the doc revived her with Narcan."

I nodded. Narcan nasal spray reversed opioid overdoses.

"She's conscious… and apparently mighty agitated," Monday said, "but we're not able to interview her yet."

Narcan worked in seconds, but Marisol would need additional doses over the next hour. "I'm glad she made it to the ER. Some police carry Narcan for emergency overdoses."

"It's not that simple, Tanaka. Carrying Narcan comes with health and liability risks. I instruct my officers to stay six feet away from an unconscious person and wait for medical personnel. Exactly what Perkins did tonight."

I was making a casual observation, but she'd taken it as a judgment on her leadership.

"Look, if you had a thing with this Montenegro woman, it's none of my business. But we found you in her hotel room along with her unconscious body."

"You can't possibly believe I would have killed her."

"I believe in facts. You argued with Nick Batista right before he collapsed. And thanks to your fentanyl tip, we took Miz Sinclair in for questioning so that Celeste Gravell could take her place and collapse herself."

"You said it, Chief. Thanks to *my* tip. Do you think I took a break during my merry murdering spree to tell you how I did it?"

"What I think is you're hiding something. You were present

for all these drug-related incidents. Add that to catching you at a Narcotics Anonymous meeting—"

"You didn't *catch* me anywhere. It was a public meeting. Since we're on the topic, what are you hiding? You have an agenda, eliciting information with deceptive tea-drinking police tactics."

Monday's smirk dropped into a neutral line. "You volunteered the info about Nick attending church. I followed up on that lead. A hot second later, you called me with your fentanyl suspicions. I followed up on that lead. Sorry if my badge and uniform confused you. And bumping into you at that meeting was a coincidence."

"Right. Your drug-addicted sister." I snorted. "What name did you give her again? Miss September?"

"January. And I'm officially no fan of sassy-tipsy Tanaka." Her jaw tensed. "Hear me when I say this—I told you the truth about that meeting." She dropped her pen and tapped the edge of the notepad against the table. "I assumed you were at that meeting playing Jessica Fletcher, but then we find you with an unconscious drug abuser."

I shrugged. Chief Malone had fooled me enough. No reason to reveal anything personal to have it used against me later. "Who called you? Perkins was banging on the door before I could dial 911."

"Who do you think?"

"Another hotel guest? Someone in the parking lot, watching the room? The actual murderer?"

"The call came from the area around the Bluebonnet Inn. The caller reported screams coming from Miz Montenegro's room."

I shook my head. "Even the television was muted. Go ask Barbara Lou for her alibi. Or is she your *mysterious* informant?"

Monday leaned forward. "Miz Sinclair is no longer a person of interest in these deaths."

"Ha! She had a bag of Nick's hair!"

"Trust that we verified her story." Monday flipped the cover of her notebook and studied me. "Officer Whales interviewed the Uncork'd bartender, who confirmed you arrived after Miz Montenegro. He also said she made an obvious pass at you. Even volunteered how he found your ride to the hotel."

"Exceptional customer service. Five stars." I tossed my head and sniffed, delivering all the Levi Blue theatrics I could muster. "If you knew I wasn't a murderer, why all these questions?"

Monday reached around to tug at her braid. "I wanted to hear it from you. Must say it surprised me you'd be with someone… like her." She flicked the braid over her shoulder. "We found more fentanyl in the hotel room. Patches. Used. In little plastic baggies pressed between the pages of the nightstand Bible."

"Marisol was hoarding used fentanyl patches? Why?"

"Someone squeezed fentanyl into Nick's nicotine patch and Celeste's sweatband. That poison came from somewhere."

So Marisol was concealing evidence of her crimes? She was also the designer of Celeste's deadly sweatband, but I kept that factoid to myself.

"What did you and Miz Montenegro talk about at the bar?" Monday asked. "She'd been drinking for a while. Was she waiting for someone? Or was your effervescent personality too irresistible?"

I lifted my cup to conceal my contemplation and contempt. Marisol had mentioned her party planner, who had gotten spooked when he saw us at the bar. Did I know the planner was male? Marisol hadn't said.

"If Marisol is the murderer, her overdose was accidental," I said. "I assumed someone rubbed her hairbrush with those patches from the trash. Have you tested the brush for fentanyl?"

"We've bagged the brush. Surprisingly, no test results have magically crossed my desk in the last hour. In the meantime, have you considered the danger you could be in?"

"Danger? I'm not connected to the victims."

"Your inadvisable snooping has disrupted this investigation. Maybe Miz Montenegro thought you were closing in, so she lured you to her hotel room—"

"Lured?" I laughed. "How would Marisol know I'd be at the wine bar? *I* didn't even know. It was a last-minute decision."

Monday shrugged. "If you're not a murderer, and you're not being set up, then you're the unluckiest man on the planet. Can you rest easily tonight on that hope?"

I hadn't considered that someone was setting me up. *Why?* Perhaps the party planner wasn't a drug dealer. Maybe it was Marisol's code for someone else. She'd mentioned something about a business transaction. Could this individual be the murderer? A bookie Vaughn referenced? The same person who killed Nick and Celeste? Did they share a connection? They played some role in the Sinclair family fitness dynasty. They were all part of the Narcotics Anonymous program. *What am I missing?*

"If you're in danger, so is your BFF. Please tell me Mayor Goofball isn't somewhere he shouldn't be."

I bristled at her nickname for Levi. "I don't know where he is. We're not exactly… It's complicated."

"Guess I missed that status update on social media." She smirked. "You're better off without him. Trust me. Once the novelty of an actor-mayor wears off, this town will fix its mistake." She sighed. "Some of the town council already have buyer's remorse. Barbara Lou Sinclair, for one."

"Levi can live with her disappointment." I picked at the lip of my paper cup. "Barbara Lou isn't too fond of law enforcement, either. And until the next mayoral election, the council handles all local appointments, including the police chief."

Monday jabbed the pen through the coil of her notepad. "I'll ask ya one more time, Tanaka. Do you know anything that'll help us find this killer? And protect you in the process?"

THE SOUNDING OF THE BELL above the door of the Cherry Blossom made me feel the most welcome I'd felt in Bluebonnet Hills.

"How'd it go?" Jenny asked.

"Go?" I blinked. "You mean… at the wine bar?"

Jenny rested her arms on the counter. "I do mean… at the wine bar. What else… could I mean?" She narrowed her eyes. "Why are you all sweaty? What's up with your hair? It's all spiky."

"I love it." Apple-cheeked Abilene looked up from her crossword puzzle. She and her twin sister were perched at the lunch counter, the only customers remaining. "Makes you look kinda rugged."

My cheeks burned, and I turned away.

"Makes you look kinda drunk." Prune-mouthed Odessa speared her after-dinner fruit cup with a fork. "I don't understand your generation. Doing everything to excess."

I opened my mouth to snark, but nothing came out except a belch of pinot grigio.

"Is Mayor Blue with you?" Abilene asked.

"I don't think so." I glanced over my shoulder to confirm. Levi popped out when he was least expected.

Abilene tapped her pencil on the crossword. "I was hoping to catch him here, you know, between second lunch and first dinner."

"We picked a good night to come." Odessa scowled at her fruit cup. "Tonight was Taste-Free Tuesday."

Confused, I looked at Jenny, who rolled her eyes. "I got a suggestion for some low-sodium specials. Guess that experiment failed."

Odessa chomped on her cantaloupe. "Fruit's all right, though."

"Ah, the power of yes in action." I chuckled, then Abilene's comment finally registered. "Levi didn't come here for dinner?"

Jenny shook her head. "Maybe he had a quiet night. Pretty sure he can at least cook soup. I showed him how to use a can opener." She swept her gaze over the nearly empty café. "I'm just finishing up here. Why don't you sit down? I'll brew some tea."

Grateful my sister sensed I wanted to be alone, I headed toward a booth in the back corner. Instead of calling from the back of a squad car, I'd texted Levi on my ride to the café. A moon icon meant Levi had activated the Do Not Disturb function, but I texted him about Marisol's near-death experience and my concerns related to Nick and Celeste's murders.

But Levi hadn't responded, and I stared at my unanswered text messages, willing a response to appear. If Monday's theory was correct, and someone was setting me up, Levi was also a target. *Should I worry? Too late.*

"You look like you need a friend."

Absently, I glanced up and smiled awkwardly at Abilene, then I peered over her shoulder.

"Odessa's taking a smoke break, and Jenny's making tea. They won't bother us." She motioned to the booth. "May I?"

I extended my hand in invitation.

"Taste-Free Tuesday." Abilene *tsk*ed over her sister's comment as she adjusted herself in the booth. "I'm surprised the nicotine hasn't killed every taste bud in that stubborn mule's mouth."

I swallowed and took a deep breath. "I—"

"Here you are, Sho-chan." Jenny placed a mug of green tea in front of me, interrupting the conversation. "Anything else I can get you, Miss Abilene?"

"I'm just keeping Sho company." She beamed up at my sister. "Dinner was wonderful tonight, Jenny. Thank you."

Jenny blushed then gauged my interest in having company.

"Thanks, sis," I said, giving my signal for the all-clear.

Satisfied, Jenny weaved her way back behind the lunch counter.

I pulled the mug closer, my fingertips flicking the string of the tea bag. "Sorry I didn't acknowledge you at the meeting," I said finally to Abilene.

"Don't apologize, dear." Her body made the booth's cushion squeak. "I sensed you were uncomfortable, and I certainly didn't want to make things worse."

"I wasn't sure what to expect, and it surprised me to see… someone like you there." I raised the mug, assessing the room for any local gossips, before sipping the tea. "How long have you been in NA? Is that… Can I ask you that?"

"Of course. I'm not embarrassed. I've been going for more than five years now. I got hooked on painkillers after my knee-re-placement surgeries."

"Does Odessa know?"

"She's the reason I'm in NA and the reason I'm still clean." Abilene leaned in. "Don't tell her that, though. She's already busting out of her britches."

I looked at my sister, who dragged a dishrag over whatever was still crusted to the lunch counter. Celeste had mentioned the importance of a support network for recovery. Abilene was confirming it.

"Celeste had been clean for fifteen years," I said. "But look at how she died. An overdose. It wasn't her fault, but the irony. She worked so hard to get her life back. What was the point? And what hope do I have of moving on with my life?"

"I don't know what you believe in, dear, but I believe He has a plan for everyone." She raised a finger to the heavens. "I know I'm just an old lady, spouting my nonsense, but Celeste did a lot of good. She helped many people. I'm proof of that. So are you. What happened to her was tragic. It's left a permanent hole in my heart. Celeste had no regrets about how she lived her life, even the bumpy parts. She left us too soon, but don't think it was for nothing."

"It was easy to talk to Celeste. Levi's the only person who knows about me. I'd never seriously considered NA or even finding a sponsor until we spoke at that meeting."

"It's truly one day at a time, Sho. That's not just a saying on a bumper sticker." She sighed and pressed back into the booth. "I thought I'd licked this thing for good myself. Even considered quitting NA." Her eyes watered. "Then my aunt Honey got sick."

A weight sank in my stomach. "You've been surrounded by a lot of death lately."

"Death is part of life," Abilene said. "No, when Honey lay in that hospice, I could barely stand to be in the same room. The doctors kept drugging her to manage the pain: IVs, patches, pills. I struggled not to swipe anything for myself or even watch the trash for carelessly discarded leftovers."

Abilene shivered at how close those thoughts had come to becoming reality. I related to that response. I took a long drink of tea to mask my pained expression.

She continued, "It's a daily struggle, managing addictions. They creep up on ya when you least expect it. The impulse to use never goes away, or at least it hasn't for me. I've just gotten better at resisting the temptation."

My phone vibrated and shook along the tabletop. The number was listed as unknown. "I should see who this is." I tapped the green button. "Hello?"

"Uh, Mr. Tanaka? It's me. Trevor. Wilkinson. From the gym. And you know, from all the murders."

"What can I do for you, Trevor?"

"It's, um, Mayor Blue. He's… kinda hanging out here."

"Hanging?" I grimaced. "Oh, must be inversion table time. After you spend more time with him, this all becomes normal."

"Right, uh, I mean, he's hanging from a tree. Outside Ms. Barbara Lou's house."

"Levi's what? Say that again?"

"Er, could you come here? Ms. Barbara Lou is super angry and wants to call the cops, and I—"

"You did the right thing calling me. I'm on my way." I glanced at the time then waved to catch Jenny's attention. "Sorry, Abilene. Can we finish our talk later?"

"Your friend needs you. Go." She retrieved a piece of paper from her purse. "Give this to Mayor Blue when you see him, will you? It's a list of all the updates I made to the *Tween of the Crime* fan wiki."

"That will cheer him up." I stuck the paper in my back pocket.

"And, Sho, dear, please don't tell the mayor what we talked about." Her eyes rested on the table. "This doesn't embarrass me, but it doesn't define me either. I wouldn't want him to lose his respect for me."

"I won't say anything." I patted her hand. "But nothing you say to Levi would change his admiration for you."

Abilene snapped her purse shut and stood. "You should take your own advice, dear."

Chapter 17

JENNY CLOSED THE CAFÉ and drove me to Barbara Lou's house. Barbara Lou stood on her top step, casting a long shadow in the moonlight. The glitter of her aurora-blue athletic wear made her twinkle when she wielded her cell at Levi.

On the bottom step, Levi jabbed his finger in the air while Lulah sat at his feet, her head volleying from her master to Barbara Lou. Trevor stood in the middle of the two feuding parties. He was shirtless, holding both hands out to mediate the ongoing firestorm.

Jenny parked her lime-green hatchback and leaned against

the steering wheel. "Uh, is this a bonus feature in the aerobics video?"

"I hope no one is filming this." My temples were already throbbing. "Don't wait up for me. Lock the front door of the café. I'll sleep at Levi's." I unbuckled my seat belt and opened the door.

"Take care of him, Sho-chan. And yourself." She shifted the car into reverse and headed toward home.

As I trotted closer to the house, I winced at the increasing intensity of the argument.

"Disgrace!" Barbara Lou shrieked. "Utter disgusting disgrace of a mayor!"

"You are the disgrace, lady," Levi said as I walked up behind him. Lulah acknowledged me with an unimpressed sniff.

When I placed my hand on Levi's shoulder, he jumped in surprise. My presence elicited the same unimpressed sniff I'd gotten from the dog.

"Your accountant is lurking in my bushes too?" Barbara Lou waved her phone at me. "I don't need tax advice!"

"Trevor called me," I said to her. "And not an accountant."

After lowering his arms, Trevor jogged the few steps to me. Sweat had made his curly hair stick to his brow, and dark stubble spread around his jawline. The moonlight made him look less fresh-faced and more hangdog. Blushing from my stare, he reached for his tank top on a nearby boulder.

"Got distracted playing referee." He slipped the tank over his head. "It's so hot out."

The consistent seventy-degree heat at almost nine p.m. was getting tiresome. I'd even made the bold choice of leaving the café blazer free. But August would arrive soon, and everyone warned I would be begging for June-level temperatures.

"Ms. Barbara Lou just popped off like a bottle rocket," Trevor said. "She's threatening to call the cops if the major doesn't resign." He watched the standoff. "I'll be in the guesthouse if you need me."

"Are… Are you living there now?"

"Super cool, huh?"

Before I could respond, Trevor trucked back to the guest-house, and I resumed his position in the line of fire. "Good evening, Barbara Lou. Sorry about the misunderstanding." I turned to Levi, who ignored me. "Perhaps if we discuss what happened, a satisfactory solution will reveal itself."

"The only *satisfactory* solution is immediate resignation," Barbara Lou said.

"Stick a leg warmer in your trap, will ya?" Levi shouted in a questionable New York accent. "I'm innocent, I tell ya. The coppers will never take me alive!"

I pulled him away from Barbara Lou. Lulah growled, nipping at my pants leg.

"What. Is. Wrong. With. You?" I asked through gritted teeth. "Do you want her to press charges? Do you want to go to jail?"

Levi tossed his head over his shoulder and yelled, "There's not a slammer that can hold me!"

"Stop it." I shook him by the elbow. "What are you doing out here?"

"Why do you care, Sho?" He yanked himself from my grip.

I shook my head. *Sho? Since when does he call me that? And why does hearing that sting?* "Because I'm your friend," I said finally. "And because you look terrible in horizontal stripes."

Levi folded his arms. "I may go to jail, but you'll always be the fashion criminal."

I studied the live oaks that loomed in front of the house. Their stately branches looked more ominous in the moonlight. "Let's exchange barbs later. Tell me why you're here, hanging from the trees."

"I was walking Lulah. My house is only a few blocks away," Levi said. "Dog walking is a totally believable cover for snooping."

"Not when you call it a cover. The police won't believe hanging from a tree branch is a common dog-walking practice."

"Branches are nature's inversion table. I was exercising while Lulah took care of business. She has a shy bladder. Don't you?" Levi bent over and rubbed the dog's head. She nuzzled his ankle.

"Clearly, you've considered all the angles."

"Psst, I'm acting." Levi narrowed his eyes. "I saw something through Barbara Lou's window. Things I can't unsee." He shivered. "I need to get into the house and look around."

"She's about to call the police, not invite you in for tea and cucumber sandwiches. What are you hoping to find?"

"Evidence. Barbara Lou did it. She killed Nick and Celeste."

I controlled the impulse to spin around and point. "How long have you been here?"

"A little less than an hour."

"Do you think Barbara Lou's been home all evening? I was in Marisol's hotel earlier. Someone tried to kill her with fentanyl."

He turned. "Her hotel room?"

"Time's up, Mayor Blue." Barbara Lou tapped her shoe against the polished concrete steps. "Am I calling the chief, or are you resigning in disgrace?"

"Let me talk to her," I said to him. "Surely there are more amenable options." I moved toward the stairs. Lulah followed on my heels. "Let's all take a deep breath."

Barbara Lou squinted at me. "I've changed my mind. Both you *and* your nosy accountant must resign in disgrace!"

"Still not an accountant!"

As if on command, Lulah collapsed on the sidewalk, pushing her hind legs out. Her tongue lolled out, and she panted heavily.

"Hold on, sweet darling. Daddy's coming." Levi rushed to the dog's side, swaying theatrically before collapsing to the ground.

"She's dehydrated. Quick—fetch two cc's of purified spring water. Stat!"

I pinched the bridge of my nose, grateful Levi had never starred in a tween medical drama.

Barbara Lou sighed, glancing at the phone in her outstretched hand. "I'll be right back."

"Wait! It's too late for water." Levi wailed. "We need to get her inside, uh, stat!"

"Inside?" Barbara Lou slipped the phone into her pocket and stepped down. "Whatever for? I'm no vet—"

"It's this sweltering Texas heat!" Levi pitched his head back and shook a fist at the sky. "Curses! Ignore the white light, sweet Lulah. Don't go toward the light!"

"Heat?" Barbara Lou looked unconvinced. "It's barely seventy degrees. Come August, you'll be begging—"

"It's the humidity!" Levi cried. "Brussels griffons like my defenseless Lulah are afflicted with flat faces." He leaned over to the panting dog and in his baby-talk voice said, "The most adorable, sweetest wittle smooshy face evah." He popped back up on his knees. "The moisture from the humidity makes her feel like she's being waterboarded again."

"Again?" Barbara Lou looked at me.

"It's an old war experience." Levi wiped away a crocodile tear. "Too painful to talk about."

Lulah rolled onto her back, raising her stubby legs to the humid Texas sky.

"Would you allow us into your kitchen for a few minutes?" I gave Barbara Lou a Scout's honor salute. "I'll babysit."

"Y'all are insane. You know that, right?"

I nodded, accepting the reality.

"If this is another stupid setup…" Her laugh bordered on hysterical. "But that would make the dog a better actor than the mayor."

I hoped we would get inside before Barbara Lou recognized the truth in her observation.

BARBARA LOU CHARGED AHEAD OF US, sweeping her arm across the papers scattered over the kitchen table. Cradling her collection, Barbara Lou widened her bug eyes at me, a signal to sit. I pulled out a chair and sat down, folding my hands into my lap.

Levi strolled in behind us, his eyes scanning across the crown molding that stretched above the walls. He bounced Lulah, who'd magically rebounded from her alleged near death by humidity.

Barbara Lou deposited the table's contents on a corner of her granite countertop before opening the cupboard door and removing a bowl. "I'll get you that water."

"Do you have any flat surfaces?" Levi asked. "Maybe a clean Frisbee? Bowls make Lulah feel like she's drowning. You know, the flat-face affliction." He stroked her coat, and I could have sworn the dog coughed for effect.

Barbara Lou cleared her throat. "No Frisbees lying around, but I have a saucer. Will that do?"

Levi bowed his head as if consulting Lulah. He eventually smiled approval for the saucer.

I shifted, noting one of the chair's legs was scraping against something other than the floor. I tugged at what looked like a brochure then laid it on the table next to me.

Barbara Lou handed the saucer to Levi, who set it in front of Lulah. She sniffed the water, yawned with disinterest, and lay down on the cool kitchen tile.

Averting my eyes from the dinner theater, I studied the brochure. Across the top panel, in pink lettering, was the phrase "Living with Breast Cancer." Bulleted lists of information accompanied stock photographs of women of various ages and ethnicities. My shoulders stiffened when I sensed Barbara Lou hovering over me. "I'm… Apologies." I didn't dare look up. "It must have fallen to the ground."

I folded my fingers underneath the chair in anticipation of being yanked from it and flung out the front door.

"No matter. The house is littered with this stuff. It multiplies like rabbits, I swear. I go to work to avoid seeing it around and thinking about it."

I nodded at the brochure. "This is for you, then?"

"If you're asking if I have breast cancer, Mr. Tanaka, the answer is yes. Every medical appointment leaves me with less clarity but more of these damn brochures. They all have the same unpronounceable words and confusing statistics."

"I don't know any Texas-based oncologists. If you'd like, I could contact a colleague in Seattle. Perhaps get a referral? There's probably a support group available through your local hospital. Your care managers could help you find one."

"That's kind, Mr. Tanaka. Really. But I've already seen seven doctors. Each one tells me something slightly different, but they all agree I'm in charge of my own treatment." She slumped into the chair across from me. "For a condition that I feel completely uninformed about."

"I hope you find a doctor that makes you comfortable. That's important for making a treatment decision."

Lulah sighed contentedly and flopped onto her side. Levi inched along the countertop to the corner where Barbara Lou had dropped the contents of her kitchen table.

"I chose a lumpectomy with radiation following the chemo." Barbara Lou drew invisible circles on the tabletop with her finger. "This was always going to be my last video. No one will watch me in a leotard after the surgery."

"Not true," I said. "You have options for reconstructive surgery. This isn't the end of your career."

"Do you know what my best quality is?" she asked.

I shook my head. Good sense prevailed, and Levi stayed silent too.

"I understand my limitations," she said. "Sure, I'm scrappy. Tough. But I know when to quit. Cancer aside, I'd been considering retirement for a while. This would have been my thirty-seventh video. What do I have to show for it? A box of VHS tapes and DVDs no one will see? The industry is changing. I've been through this before, but this time feels different. My attempts to keep going, maybe reinvent myself, are all failing. Epically."

I lowered my eyes. "You mean the... the strip-aerobics idea?"

Barbara Lou chuckled. "That, yes, but I meant partnering with Nicky. I've spent most of my career on my own, convincing myself that was best for me. But once I found a solid partner, someone I could mold and learn from, well, I foolishly believed I could work longer."

"And Nick was that partner?" Levi's attention was focused downward.

"Nicky had undeniable charisma in front of the camera." Barbara Lou hadn't noticed Levi's new position. "He introduced my fitness philosophy to people who'd never have watched me otherwise." She waved a hand at me. "Men, for one. Working with Nicky showed me I'd focused too much on keeping up with the trends and lost my core audience."

"What you told us after Nick's death was true," Levi said. "At least partially. But you didn't just want Nick to continue your legacy. You wanted to keep that legacy in the family." Levi held up a box with rainbow-colored packaging.

The box was a saliva test kit from one of those mail-in DNA genetic testing companies.

Levi asked, "When did you first suspect Nick was your son?"

Her eyes widened. Again, I braced myself for the sonic boom.

Instead, Barbara Lou melted deeper into her chair, unburdened from a heavy secret.

"The first moment I saw him," she said. "It was in his face. My Pablo was in there." She sighed. "Took my breath away."

"Pablo Alvarado?" I clarified. "The high school football star who married Celeste?"

"He was mine before Celeste sank her fangs into him." Barbara Lou glared at me. "Celeste took away everything that belonged to me. Everything. Pablo and I planned to elope after graduation. Celeste had other plans, and…" She stabbed a finger into the table. "After Celeste squeezed what she wanted from Pablo, she moved to the next target."

"Vaughn?" I asked.

"Then to the next."

"Nick."

"When I met Nicky, he was a husk of himself. Gaunt, strung out. His teeth were soft and black like rotted fruit. I took a risk by hiring him and asking him to live here. But I thought he had something, and I was right. I introduced him to the therapeutic benefits of exercise, something I'd relied on with my weight battles and depression. And Nicky cleaned himself up. He started setting goals and channeling his ambition."

"It made you proud to watch," Levi said.

Barbara Lou nodded. "Celeste swooped in with her motherly facade. She wanted to fix him and make him atone. But his life experiences gave him his authenticity and edge. When that twit Marisol burst into his life, she tried to mold him into her ideal fitness personality. Some caricature with no connection to his fans. Those aren't the marks for a sustainable career. That's not what I wanted for Nicky."

"You were protecting him?" I asked. Was this leading to a murder confession?

"I tried. But Nicky wanted to leave me. He'd gotten what he needed." She laughed softly. "I loved what he'd become, but his success was at my expense."

"He was about to sign an exclusive contract with Marisol," Levi said.

"He wanted me to join him, but my heart wasn't in it." She sniffed and wiped her eyes. "And now, with Nicky gone, there's nothing left to do. Accept my limitations and retire."

I asked, "And was he? Your son?"

Barbara Lou slapped her hands on the table. "I was never exactly sure how to have that conversation. Nicky confessed he'd been adopted but was vague about the details. Well, I'm sure he shared with Celeste." She laughed bitterly. "Nicky never expressed an interest in finding his birth parents, but I needed to know. I even rummaged through his things, looking for a birth certificate, adoption records, or something that held the truth. The DNA test was my last gasp of desperation, but I couldn't figure out a way to get him to take it."

Lulah released a loud snore, the hair above her eyes swaying slightly.

"She seems sufficiently hydrated. If you'll excuse me." Barbara Lou stood and smoothed the fabric of her athletic wear. "I was on my way to work out when I caught the peeping mayor outside my window. After our little chat, I'd like to release some of this tension before I explode." Her eyes bugged when she removed her phone from her pocket. "Unless you'd still like me to make that phone call, Mayor Blue?"

Chapter 18

"**D**ID SHE JUST CONFESS TO MURDER?" I asked once we were outside Barbara Lou's house.

Levi set down Lulah, who trotted down the steps in search of some shrubs. "Clearly, she resented Celeste and Marisol for interfering with her relationship with Nick. Why kill Nick, though?"

I stared at my feet as we walked down the steps. "If she couldn't have him, no one could? Sounds extreme, but she lost her fiancé and her son. Then the cancer diagnosis. Losing Nick might have finally broken her."

"Why fentanyl? Where would she have gotten that? Her oncologist?"

"Some medical research suggests fentanyl promotes cell generation. And the patches are used to reduce cancer-related pain. But she's too early in the treatment process for fentanyl."

"She got it from somewhere. I don't see Barbara Lou socializing with drug dealers, even out of desperation."

"I did." I breathed in the evening air, listening to Lulah snort among the flowers and bushes. "What made you suspect Nick was her son? That's what brought you here tonight, right?"

He gave a curt nod. "I kept thinking about that bag of Nick's hair. Why carry it around? It was odd enough that it must've meant something to her. I remembered what Marisol said outside the church."

I searched my memory. Seeing Marisol with Celeste on those church steps had led me to that meeting. It was also where my inadvertent tip to the police had gotten me into hot water with Levi, a topic we hadn't revisited yet.

"That's right. Marisol caught Barbara Lou rummaging through Nick's trash. Something about bagging a Q-tip?" I tapped my chin. "Perhaps Barbara Lou tried testing DNA from an ear swab. You can get DNA from hair follicles, so the bag of hair fits your theory too. Though I doubt labs would have been able or willing to test either."

"Barbara Lou wanted Nick to spit into a test tube for a mail-in genealogy test. She explored every option." Levi turned away and stepped into the darkness of the front yard.

"That's illegal," I said. "Doing a DNA test without consent."

"You think Barbara Lou cares about legalities?"

I cleared my throat. "Look, Levi, uh, about earlier—"

"C'mon." His voice grew distant as he disappeared around the side of the house.

I glanced at the porch light above Barbara Lou's door before slipping into the blackness behind Levi.

He pulled open the wrought-iron gate that led into Barbara Lou's backyard. "It's unlocked. Trevor wants to talk to us."

"How do you know that?" I followed Levi through the gate and noticed the dim lighting in the guesthouse.

"When I told you I saw things through Barbara Lou's window? Things I can't unsee? Trevor was one of those things." Levi rapped on the door and pushed it open. Lulah came panting from behind and streaked through the front door.

Trevor balled a clean pair of socks and tossed them into a basket on the floor. "Is… Is she gone yet?"

"Barbara Lou? She mentioned wanting to work out."

Trevor scooted around the table that divided the living room from the kitchen and grabbed two glasses from a cabinet. "I'm super grateful you showed up, Mayor Blue. I don't know what would've happened if she hadn't caught you hanging outside her window."

"What did happen?" Levi settled in a recliner and swiveled around to face Trevor. Lulah batted a paw against Levi's leg, a signal to let her into his lap.

"Ms. Barbara Lou asked me to clean out the basement." Trevor removed a water pitcher from the refrigerator and filled the glasses. "She said I could work out there. But there were boxes stacked everywhere and clothes hanging off equipment."

I moved away from the windows and lingered in front of a corner shelf crammed with framed photos and fitness books: *How to Become a Successful Personal Trainer* and Arnold Schwarzenegger's *Encyclopedia of Modern Bodybuilding*.

Trevor continued, "After I'd been cleaning for a few hours, Barbara Lou told me to take a break. She wanted me to see something."

"Is that why your shirt was off?" I asked.

He handed me a water glass and set Levi's on the card table

next to his recliner. "It was hot in that basement. Anyway, Barbara Lou asked me for feedback on her new routine, and, well, she just started… dancing."

"That wasn't dancing." Levi rocked in the recliner, scratching the ear of a snoring Lulah. "It was full-on twerking."

"Full-on what-ing?" I asked.

"Twerking," Trevor said. "You know, that dance move where you squat and work your hips." He smacked his hands on his thighs in demonstration.

I set down my water glass and waved at him to stop. "I get it. There's not enough bleach to erase the mental image."

My eyes landed on a framed photo on one of the corner shelves. Trevor, perhaps seven or eight years old, grinned at the camera, holding a stuffed shark. A man with an equally bright smile had his arm wrapped around Trevor, his lips pressed into Trevor's cheek. He also had curly brown hair, so I placed him as Trevor's deceased father.

The parent-child image made sense to me, especially compared to the strange dynamic between Barbara Lou and Nick. If Trevor craved a parental figure, I feared he got more than he wanted with Barbara Lou.

"Why did you move in here if you were already aware of Barbara Lou's behavior?"

"I mean, she took it to the limit tonight. Before, she'd check me out at the gym. Like when I'd bent over and cleaned equipment. Or when she saw me lifting, she'd stay stuff like 'Delicious progress, Trev.'"

I remembered being on the stair-climber and seeing Barbara Lou ogling Trevor. She wasn't subtle about it. Returning my focus to the photo of Trevor and his father, I sighed. "Do your classes begin in the fall? At the community college?"

"I haven't had time to finish the admissions paperwork. I've been slammed at work and, you know, getting to do things like the video."

"No rush. The spring semester will be here before you know it."

"Yeah, maybe. I mean, there are a few certifications I could get for training and stuff. Barbara Lou said the gym would pay for it. I might do that instead."

"Oh. I thought you said certifications were meaningless."

"What's that supposed to mean?" Trevor asked.

"Uh, sorry. I thought that's how you described them." I smiled. "Whatever you decide, things appear to be working out. More important, the police seem less interested in you as a murder suspect. Have they interviewed you again?"

"Not since Celeste died. When they talked to everyone." Trevor relaxed in his chair. "I moved here to feel safe. Now I'm not so sure it was a good choice. Do you think I'm safe here?"

"Safe from the police?" Levi asked.

"I guess, and from Barbara Lou."

"You think what happened tonight was more than harmless flirting?"

It appeared Barbara Lou had transferred her attention from Nick to Trevor. She'd gone from taking Nick lunch at work to showcasing seductive dance moves for Trevor. When Trevor came to us, he'd described his dream of going to college. It appeared he'd traded that dream for a few certifications at Barbara Lou's expense. Perhaps that was the more practical decision. Trevor would continue to gain experience in an area he loved without racking up student loan debt. I wondered, though, if Barbara Lou expected payment for the newfound hospitality, and Trevor was questioning his decisions.

"It's like that episode of *Tween of the Crime*," Trevor said to Levi. "You took that sweet girl to the prom. But when you gave her the corsage, she jammed it into your mouth. Then she was all sweet again until she dumped punch down your pants. You eventually figured out they were evil twins seeking revenge for voting against their proposed prom theme."

Levi scratched his chin. "Yin and Yang. They opposed the theme 'One Night in Bangkok.'" He shrugged. "It was a very culturally sensitive episode, Sho."

There it is again. Sho.

Trevor chuckled. "No, Mayor Blue. The evil twins in that episode were Polka and Dot. Remember? They were the European folk artists who yodeled you into a dance trance."

Levi raised a finger in the air and let it sink back down. "Hmm. Right again, Trev. My memory isn't what it used to be."

I remembered the list of *Tween of the Crime* wiki updates Abilene had given me. Perhaps a cheat sheet would help Levi hold on to his memories. "Nostalgia aside, Trevor. How's that related to your safety concerns?"

He shrugged and stood, noticing my interest in his photos. "Just that Barbara Lou acted one way when she hired me. And now she's acting another." He raised an eyebrow in Levi's direction. "Maybe she's got an evil twin."

Levi smiled thinly, but his face froze in defeat.

Trevor moved beside me, adjusting the photo of him and his dad. "I still miss him. All the time."

When I lowered my eyes, I spotted another photo. "Who's that? Your mother?" I pointed to a woman wearing a bright floral leotard and standing next to a sullen Trevor. The photo looked recent, and the contrast between Trevor's expression there and the one with his dad was striking.

"My aunt." Trevor bent over and handed me the picture. "I lived with her after Dad... Until I turned eighteen."

"Did you get some of your fitness interest from her?"

"Not even a little." Trevor laughed. "She exercised, but her

fitness plan couldn't burn the calories from a daily brisket plate."
He reached for the photo and ran his finger across the glass.
"Guess I shouldn't say stuff like that. I mean, she was a fan of
Ms. Barbara Lou's. That's how I learned about aerobics and where
Bluebonnet Hills was." He repositioned the frame on the shelf.
"Guess it wasn't all bad."

The sound of a car engine turning over made us freeze and
listen. Gravel popped against rubber tires, and the hum of the
engine disappeared in the distance.

Trevor released a deep sigh, relief washing over his face.
"I hope she finds what she's looking for."

"What do you mean, Trev?" Levi asked.

Trevor lifted the laundry basket. "She wants some video
footage from the day Nick died."

"She wants something to remember him by?"

"Um, that's not how it sounded." Trevor's face crinkled. "It's
that B-roll footage the interns took. You know, that behind-the-
scenes stuff they add to make everyone seem relatable?"

"Couldn't she ask Vaughn for that?" I asked. "She owns all
that footage anyway."

Trevor shrugged. "She asked me to go into Vaughn's office
tonight and grab it. I told her I wouldn't do that." He froze and
looked up at the ceiling. "Barbara Lou wasn't going to call the
cops on you, Mayor Blue. She wanted to get that footage."

Levi rose from the recliner so abruptly that it continued to
rock without him. Lulah's ears perked up, her nap disrupted.
"What was on that video?"

"Something so interesting that she's on her way to the Lone
Star to find it," I said.

OUR HOT PURSUIT OF BARBARA LOU cooled rather quickly.

After we left Trevor's guesthouse, it took us about ten minutes to hustle back to Levi's place. He didn't have an extra Segway for me, and I held my ground on riding with him on his.

Instead, I chose a perfectly acceptable bike, forgetting that Segways didn't need to be pedaled. The trip was the most exercise I'd had in a while, and though I'd already sobered a bit after the three glasses of pinot, it took me the rest of the way.

"Now what?" I asked when we arrived at the gym. Barbara Lou's SUV was in the parking lot, which was otherwise empty. "Do we just stroll on in and ask to see the footage?"

Levi gave a defeated sigh. Lulah popped her head up from her basket to investigate the commotion.

"Hold on," I said. "Let's try that emergency exit door with the fickle lock, the one that leads into the men's locker room."

Levi maneuvered the Segway in that direction, and I pedaled behind him. When we arrived, I got off the bike and rested it against the brick exterior.

"You stay here, girl." Levi slipped the dog some treats. "This is like the third act of every *Tween of the Crime* episode. Right before I unmasked the villain and restored tween justice."

I gulped. "How many times did you get arrested for breaking and entering?"

"Our writers didn't worry about things like police procedure. Too constraining."

I slowly pressed down on the door handle and heard the click. "Hmm. Okay, here's the plan. I left my phone in the locker room the last time we were here, and I came by to pick it up and saw the door open."

"Now look who's concocting cover stories for snooping." It was the first time I'd heard Levi laugh that night. "And the locker room leads into the hallway across from Vaughn's office. Maybe we can slip in, watch the footage, and slip back out."

"Maybe…" But saying it out loud didn't convince me.

We practically tiptoed into the locker room. I pulled the door closed behind me, and we both breathed a sigh of relief—until the eco-friendly lights above us clicked on.

"Don't move," I said through my teeth. "New plan, new plan. Those lights are motion sensitive. We'll leave a well-lit path all the way to Vaughn's office."

Levi raised his hands to his side and slowly lowered himself to the ground.

"What are you doing?" I hissed.

"Trying Plan B." Once he'd squatted on the ground, Levi fell forward, his hands catching his fall, then he sprawled across the tile floor.

I sucked air through my teeth. "Now what?"

Using his hands, Levi pulled himself across the tile. Then he pushed off with his boots to slide farther.

"Keep going," I said. "See if you activate the next light."

Levi glided across the floor. The lights stayed off. "I think this'll work."

Slowly, I squatted down to the tile. My calves still burned from the bike ride, so that movement didn't help. When I reached the ground, I tipped forward and smacked into the tile.

"You okay?" Levi pulled himself farther.

I groaned before sucking it up and inching behind him. Pressing my cheek into the cool tile, I relied on the scraping from Levi's boots to guide me out of the locker room.

Eventually, my fingers grabbed the rubber strip that transitioned the tile of the locker room to the carpet of the gym's interior. I lifted my cheek from the tile and pulled myself forward, careful not to scrape my chin.

As we crawled, a *swish* came from my right. "What's that sound?" I asked the heels of Levi's boots.

Levi stopped, listened, and craned his neck around to look at me. "Cardio bike. Barbara Lou must be exercising."

The reality of what we were doing washed down my body and punched me in the gut. But Levi continued to pull ahead to Vaughn's office, and turning back seemed like too much effort.

Levi made it to Vaughn's office, stopping to hold his head upright and confirm that, yes, every area in the gym was wired with those motion lights. He crawled around the corner to Vaughn's desk, sliding along the plastic chair mat and rolling the chair to the side. I slid next to him until we were elbow to elbow. We both raised our heads to the computer monitor, which loomed above us, and groaned.

"Now what?" The green light and the running fan showed the computer was on, but I didn't know how to access the footage.

"Don't move." Levi slowly raised his hand into the air. "I have a plan."

"What if the plan fails?"

"Run."

Levi's hand fumbled in the air. Eventually, he lowered Vaughn's wireless keyboard to the ground.

"Brilliant," I said.

Levi hit Enter, and we were prompted for a password. Our groan chorus continued.

"Any guesses?" Levi asked. "BarbieDreamhouse? Fitness4Evah?"

I blew a breath through my nostrils. "Try Spielberg."

Levi used his pointer finger to press each key. Then he hit Enter, and we held our breath.

"Eureka," Levi said.

"We make a great team."

"Hmm." Levi craned his neck to study the desktop. "Now what?" He pressed the tab key to toggle over the names of various desktop folders.

"Use that search bar. In the bottom left corner. You should be able to search for files by date."

After what seemed like an hour, Levi had typed the date of the first aerobics shoot into the search bar. A screen with a list of files with .mp4 extensions appeared.

I sighed. "Click on the first one and go from there."

The first file loaded to show an image of Nick, his capped teeth flashing at the camera, doing a little silly muscle flexing. It looked like it'd been shot before we'd arrived. I heard Nick's voice, but it sounded muffled.

Ugh, the volume. I hadn't accounted for that.

"Vaughn's got headphones plugged into the computer," Levi said, presumably reading my thoughts. He pointed at them. "Barbara Lou can't hear us."

The footage of Nick ended.

"That's it?" I bonked my forehead against the plastic chair mat.

"For that file, anyway." Levi clicked on the second video file. "There's us!"

Yikes. There I was in my Ojii-chan's tracksuit, trying to follow Celeste's moves.

"Is he wearing that?" The voice came from behind the camera. It sounded like Nick, but Levi was closer to the headphones.

"I asked them to wear their own clothes," Ramona said. "You should see the mayor."

Levi clicked his tongue. "I looked quite festive."

"Just stick 'em in the back," Nick replied. "No one will notice those clowns anyway."

The video faded to black.

"Rude, but it doesn't tell us anything new," I said.

Levi sighed and clicked on the third file. Barbara Lou's shriek ripped through the headphones, causing me to jump and raise my head to ensure she hadn't snuck up on us.

"This was when she yelled at that intern for filming her," Levi said. "So temperamental."

"Wait. Stop that. Can you rewind and play it again?"

Levi toggled over to the pause button and clicked an arrow that rewound the video by several seconds.

"There," I said. "She's putting something into her duffel. That's why she's screeching at the intern. He surprised her."

"What is that?" Levi stretched his neck up to get closer to the monitor.

"White paper or… patches. Those are the patches, Levi. That's how she got away with it. She slipped the poisoned patch to Nick and carried the rest out in her duffel bag."

"But the police searched everything."

I shook my head. "Remember how Barbara Lou got hysterical when Nick collapsed? I mean, I was preoccupied with my panic attack, but I remember the screaming."

Levi gasped. "Your panic attack gave Barbara Lou cover. That plus Nick collapsing distracted everyone enough for her to slip out, toss the duffel somewhere, and slip back in."

"Just in time to accuse me of murder," I said.

"She's sunshine and rainbows," Levi said. He slipped his hand into his pocket and pulled out his phone.

"Who are you calling?"

Levi rolled onto his back with a laugh. "I'm documenting evidence." He craned the phone around, activated the VIDEO function, and replayed the video of Barbara Lou.

"Now what?" I asked when Levi finished making the video. "Do we jump out and accuse Barbara Lou of murder?"

"No reception in here." Levi slipped the phone back into his pocket. "I'll deny this if you repeat it, but let's crawl back, find a signal, and text this evidence to Chief Malone. I'm tired."

That was the most logical thing I'd ever heard Levi say. The knot in my stomach tightened.

Chapter 19

WE CRAWLED FROM VAUGHN'S OFFICE and back toward the locker room. I dragged myself across the carpet, noticing the absence of any swooshing sounds from Barbara Lou's stationary bike.

Had she already seen the footage? Why didn't she erased it? In our haste to flee the office, we'd neglected to check the computer's recycle bin for deleted files. Was there other evidence incriminating Barbara Lou?

I stopped to catch my breath and contemplated returning to the office. I almost called to Levi, but his boots were pulling farther and farther away. He'd almost reached the locker room, an archway of light welcoming his return.

Wait. Who turned on the lights? Did I activate them when I crawled across the transition into the hallway?

Planting my palms on the carpet, I pushed myself above Levi's slithering body. All the lights in the locker room were on. Was Barbara Lou waiting for us?

The lights above the cardio station clicked off, and an air vent above me clicked on. My fatigued muscles gave out and pushed me to the floor.

Levi stood and noticed the light bulb above his head. His eyes landed on me before he turned and disappeared into the locker room.

I moved as quickly as I could, careful not to activate any lights in the gym area. When my fingertips hit the cold locker room tile, I pulled myself forward, slid inside, and stumbled up after Levi.

Levi came from behind the shower area. "There's no one here now."

I turned my head toward the wooden benches and rows of lockers. Everything looked as it normally did. Then my gaze landed on the steam room door, which was hanging open. I pointed it out to Levi, who was closer to it than I was.

Levi grabbed the handle and pulled the door open farther.

"Something's in there." I stepped toward the door, squinting to recognize what was lying on the tiled bench.

Taking a breath, I stepped inside and moved to the corner. A royal-blue sweatband and leg warmers lay there.

"Are those Celeste's? She was wearing them when she collapsed." Levi had followed me and held his hand out to the objects.

"Don't touch," I said. "They could be poisoned."

The door behind us banged shut, and grunting came from behind the frosted glass.

"What the…"

Steam hissed around us, misting my clothes. I hustled to the door and pushed on it, then turned and thrust my shoulder into the handle. We'd been locked in.

Levi pointed at the sweatband and legwarmers. "If those suckers are soaked in fentanyl, we have about five seconds left."

I slid my fingers along the doorframe, searching for a latch or safety release. "Do you see anything we could use to break the glass?" The steam billowed around us.

Levi pulled off his boots and chucked one at the door, but it bounced off the glass. I turned the other boot around and banged the heel against the glass to no avail.

"Guess these weren't poisoned." Levi picked up the sweatband and sat on the bench. "We'd be dead by now."

I continued to bang the boot heel into the glass. "Then we have dehydration and heat stroke to look forward to."

"Think of all the toxins we're sweating out. Our skin will look amazing."

"Open caskets for all!" I continued to bang the boot against the glass but made no progress.

Levi glanced at his phone. "No bars. Guess steam rooms weren't built for good cell reception."

"How can you be so calm?"

"I've been through this before." He smiled. "In the pilot of *Tween of the Crime*."

"Of course you were." Defeated, I hurled the boot to the ground.

"In the act three finale, I got locked in a steam room with Nanny Haberdashery, my very English sidekick. We were trapped by Suki St. Shiatsu, a germophobe masseuse who went insane from the cabbage-soup diet."

"Sounds like another authentic representation of Asians."

"It was a very topical episode. The cabbage-soup diet had

taken the country by storm, but no one discussed the enzyme released in cooked cabbage that caused insanity."

"Perhaps because there isn't one?"

"To save me, Nanny shattered the steam-room door with the business end of her parasol. She made the ultimate sacrifice, reaching through the shards of glass to turn off the steam."

I sighed. "Very heroic. Where's the sacrifice? Did she get cut?"

Levi lowered his eyes. "Suki St. Shiatsu had also fed cabbage soup to her Pekingese, Chuck. Naturally, the enzyme turned Chuck feral. He must have mistaken Nanny's fingers for Vienna sausages, and…."

This is how I'm going to die—steamed like a bag of peas while being tortured with Tween of the Crime *episode descriptions.*

"Chuck nipped off Nanny's pointer finger," Levi said. "We revisited that in a season-three story arc."

"What's the point of all this?"

"Point? Oh, I forget you need those." Levi cocked his head. "Nanny threw me to the floor to avoid the steam. Apparently, heat rises."

He was right, of course, fueling further annoyance. I flattened myself on the few-degrees-cooler tile. It wouldn't save us, but it might provide a few extra minutes to devise a plan.

Levi lay down in front of me. "Your skin is glowing, by the way."

I twisted my head and let my cheek sink to the tile. "I'm sorry. For whatever that's worth. I should have shared my theories. Walking into that meeting—and discovering I belonged there—scared me."

"Do you really not have a bucket list? Nothing you want to do before you die?"

"Learning poker always intrigued me. It's a game of strategy that requires quick decision making."

"Vegas road trip, baby! That place is one big Hollywood

sound stage. Colorful lights, eccentric people, showbiz… and the buffets." Levi groaned. "A literal buffet of buffets."

"I'm not interested in sneeze guards and the Blue Man Group. I'd prefer to play poker at home against the computer. I bet it's pretty satisfying when you beat it."

"I forgot about finding you a hobby." Levi sighed. "Do you know why this investigation is important to me? Not because I hope it'll reboot my show."

"Sorry about saying that too." I pressed my lips together. They were surprisingly supple. "Because you wanted to help Trevor?"

"Listening to him talk about his dad brought back memories of mine. Our father-son thing was joke shops. We loved Gag Me with a Spoon on Hollywood Boulevard. Owned by a guy called Mr. Pinky."

"Hmm, are you sure that wasn't one of your show's super villains?"

"Everyone who walked into the store got Mr. Pinky's customary greeting—an invitation to smell his flower corsage, which shot invisible ink into your face."

"I understand people prefer that to handshakes or air kisses."

"Dad seemed different that day, more cautious. We'd made that trip along Hollywood Boulevard hundreds of times, but he acted like it was the first. He and Mr. Pinky went way back, so when Dad bent over to smell the rose, I thought he was playing along with the bit."

"He wasn't."

"Mr. Pinky brayed like a donkey. He thought Dad was acting too. Until Dad balled his fists, and I hustled him out of there. He deteriorated pretty quickly after that. We never went to another joke shop."

"Those final stages of dementia are tough on patients and their families," I said. "I've been dismissive about your bucket list. You want a full life. No regrets."

"The anxiety of inheriting his disease crushes me, Tanaka-san. Every time I forget something, I wonder if it's an early sign of what's to come. What we're doing now is more exciting than any acting gig. But none of it's worth experiencing if I forget it all someday. I need a deputy to remind me."

"You can count on me." My cheek slurped like a plunger when I lifted from the tile. "I already regret asking, but wasn't Nanny Poppycock your very English sidekick?"

"Nanny Haberdashery's act of courage painted the writers into a corner. Tween viewers would never accept a sidekick with no pointer finger. How could she scold suspects?"

"Tolerant fans."

"Our second episode opened with Nanny Haberdashery being struck by a beer truck on her way to pick up some pain medication. It served as a kind of one-two PSA for alcohol and drug prevention."

"You're making that up."

"Season one, episode two: 'No Laughing Splatter.'"

"That reminds me…" I dug into my back pocket and removed the list Abilene had given me. "The ink's probably running, but here are the updates to your *Tween of the Crime* fan wiki."

Levi stuck the list into the boot lying next to him. "At least the wiki lives in perpetuity. Even if we don't."

We lay in silence on the steam room floor, my face almost melting into the tile. My eyelids grew heavy, and the idea of a nap made sense. Perhaps it would help me think of a way to get us out of there.

Something coarse brushed against my eyelid. I flinched and batted the air, feeling a rough texture—fur.

I opened my eyes, and a flat-faced Brussels griffon blinked at me. The hissing from the steam had stopped, and flushes of cold air swept over my body. The door to the steam room was open.

"Levi." I pushed myself up to a sitting position and wiped the steam off my face. "Somebody turned off the steam. We're alive."

Levi rolled to his side, swinging his long legs to get into an upright position. "Of course. Heroes never get steamed. Classic trope." He pulled Lulah to him to snuggle, glanced at the door, and gasped.

Barbara Lou hovered above us, and I stared into the whites of her big bug eyes.

"It was you all along." I stumbled up from the floor to confront Barbara Lou. "Well, we've got you now, sister. The jig is up! Levi, show her the video."

Levi sprang up and dug out his phone. "Uh. My phone got a little poached from the steam." He held out his hand. "You got a bag of rice?"

"A bag of...?"

"I need to submerge the phone in rice immediately. You think there's some at the café?"

"Uh, probably."

Levi shook the phone at Barbara Lou. "You just wait. Sister. Because in forty-eight hours... minimum... your reign of terror will be over."

I held the back of my hand over my mouth. "We could always get the video directly off the computer."

"Good idea," Levi said. "Amazing she didn't just delete the file."

"You know, I thought the same thing."

Levi chuckled. "Criminals always trip up on those tiny details. Think we could submit this to that TV show about dumb criminals?"

"What are you two morons blathering about?" Barbara Lou's beet-red face and puffed cheeks resembled a tea kettle.

I tilted my head as I realized Barbara Lou was practically

naked, wrapped in a towel. Odd choice to wear to a murder. Of course, what did one wear to a murder?

"And what video?" Barbara Lou continued. "How did you dum-dums even get in here?"

Levi and I exchanged confused glances.

"I just saved your bacon," she said. "Lulah barked her way into my locker room and led me here. Someone had wedged a mop against the door."

"You're not here to murder us?" I asked.

"I'm keeping my options open." Barbara Lou clicked her tongue at Levi. "I should have called the chief. You truly are a disgrace to this town."

I scratched my head. "I... So, if you're not here to murder us, what are you doing here? Wrapped in a towel?"

A muscle in Barbara Lou's jaw tensed. "I wanted to use the steam room."

Levi cackled. "Ha, unlikely story. We won't be tricked by your nonsensicalness. This is the *men's* locker room!"

Barbara Lou blinked. "After hours. In the gym. That I own. Besides, I prefer the pressure in here."

"Oh." Levi stumbled backward and picked up his boot.

"Hold on here." I shook my head. "We saw the video. The footage of you hiding the nicotine patches in your duffel. You were discarding the murder weapon."

"*That...?* You're just as dense as the other one. I wasn't discarding anything. I took those patches away from Nicky." She sniffed. "Our fitness shoots always stressed him out. Nicotine wasn't the solution."

I sighed, clearer thoughts prevailing. "You were protecting him. Again. You didn't want Nick using another drug to deal with his issues."

Barbara Lou's mouth puckered before she spun around to leave.

"Where are you going?" I tripped out of the steam room.

"To fetch my phone. To call Chief Malone. This charade ends tonight. For the sake of this town."

"Wait. If you're not the murderer, someone else still is."

Levi limped out of the steam room with one boot on. He withdrew the list I'd given him from the other boot before slipping it on. Lulah plopped down on the tile in front of him.

"Catching a murderer isn't my immediate concern, Mr. Tanaka. Ridding Bluebonnet Hills of this clown-show mayor is."

"You didn't come here tonight to erase that video?"

"*What* video?" Barbara Lou began to wave her hands but quickly dropped them to secure the towel. "I still don't know what you're talking about."

"Oh. My…" My jaw fell slack. "This was a trap. We were lured here. Levi, we were played. It was—"

"Yin and Yang." Levi waved the list of wiki updates. "Yin *and* Yang. Yin. And. Yang. Yin and Yang!"

"He's talking in tongues." Barbara Lou stepped backward. "He's finally cracked."

I tensed. "No. He's having the same realization I am."

Levi scanned a finger down the list. "And it *was* Professor Killjoy. Major Wet Noodle, my left foot." He smacked the list against his palm. "He's never even watched my show!"

"Perhaps not the key takeaway here."

Barbara Lou stamped her foot. "Who are you talking about? What's going on here?"

Lulah released a low growl, extending her front paws. We all watched her.

"Easy, girl," Levi said. "What do you see?"

Lulah advanced a few more steps, her fur spiking at attention.

Barbara Lou took another step back. "That dog has never liked me. You must have trained her to think I'm a murderer."

"I don't think she's growling at you," I said.

Though Lulah took two steps forward for every one Barbara Lou took backward.

"She senses something." Levi leaned sideways, toward the locker room exit.

Holding her position, Lulah barked. Barbara Lou took another step back. Suddenly, Lulah bolted out of the locker room, zooming past Barbara Lou, who yelped and attempted to clear the dog's path, only to trip over her feet and fall to the ground.

"Hold on, sweet baby," Levi called. "Daddy's coming."

"Levi, don't! He could be out there."

Ignoring me, Levi leaped over a sprawled-out Barbara Lou and ran into the gym.

As I looked down at a whimpering Barbara Lou, my first impulse was to grab another towel and toss it to her. My aim was better than I'd thought, though I tossed it over her head. Barbara Lou flailed her arms, resembling a peevish ghost.

"Don't try to stand." I crouched and observed the swelling around her ankle. "Where's your phone?"

Barbara Lou winced as I adjusted her foot to a more comfortable angle. "In my locker."

"I want to elevate this first." I looked at the wooden benches near the lockers.

"I can't make it over there. In a towel." Barbara Lou had read my thoughts.

I scanned the locker room exit, searching for any signs of Levi or Lulah, but saw nothing. Then I turned back toward the steam room and the shelf where I'd grabbed the extra towels. I jumped up and grabbed a stack of towels and propped Barbara Lou's ankle on it.

"If you can't make it to my locker," she said, "there's a phone in Vaughn's office and one at the front desk."

"Thanks. Uh… don't move."

Barbara Lou snarled, "Thanks for the tip, Nurse Nightingale."

Chapter 20

BREATHE, I TOLD MYSELF. *Name five things you can see.*
One: Vaughn's office.

Abandoning a snarky Barbara Lou on the floor of the men's locker room was an effortless decision. I bounded toward Vaughn's office in search of his phone.

Keep moving. Do not stop to think, to analyze. Do. Not. Panic.

The motion-sensor lights in Vaughn's office illuminated a chaotic desk. Still, Barbara Lou had said a phone was there somewhere.

I gingerly lifted a folder from the desk and tossed it to the ground. At that pace, I would find the phone by morning. Using both hands, I tugged at various folders and papers, jerking them off the desk and throwing them to the floor.

Breathe. Name five things you can see. One: Vaughn's office. Two: a glass ashtray of cigarette butts. I grabbed the ashtray, which bumped against something hard. *A phone?* I moved the heavy ashtray to the other side of the desk and clawed through the scattered pieces of paper.

Breathe. Breathe. Name five things you can see.

Three: The base of a phone.

I blinked at the telephone base, which had a missing receiver and cord.

"Clever little punk." I pounded my fist into the phone base.

If Trevor had taken the handset from Vaughn's office, he'd probably done the same at the front desk. I could dash into the women's locker room for Barbara Lou's phone. *But how much time am I losing?*

Perhaps I should leave the gym and go to the police. Of course, I would either have to pedal there or take Levi's Segway. The bike would get me to the station faster, but I didn't think my calves would last.

When this is over, you're getting a job. And a car. No more green transportation.

Wait. Barbara Lou wasn't green. She was an everyday suburbanite who drove a gas-guzzling SUV. I would take her car.

Keys. Where are her keys? She likely didn't have them hiding in her towel, so I would still have to go to the women's locker room.

I gripped the edge of Vaughn's desk, staring through the glass that enclosed his office. All the lights in the gym were on.

That had to look suspicious to somebody, right? Perhaps Officer Perkins would notice them while on evening patrol.

Breathe. I can do this.

Do not panic. Name five things you can see.

"Office. Ashtray. Phone. The top of Levi's head." I blinked. "The top of Levi's head?"

Yet there it was. His messy textured hair bobbed into view and disappeared again. And again. And again.

I slogged around Vaughn's desk, tripping over the mounds of paper I'd flung, and into the gym, then trotted into the cardio area, where machines whirred.

The frames of the sleek black cardio equipment—ellipticals, stationary bikes, and treadmills—obstructed my view, but if I pitched back my head… there was Levi, at the top of an eight-foot stair-climber. His hands were bound with something pink and rubber.

"You're always telling me to exercise more." Levi slouched over the rails of the machine, his boots clomping against the rotating stairs.

"How did you even get up there?"

"It's a sordid tale involving a deception trail of bacon."

I shook my head. "Is that Marisol's resistance band you're tied up with?"

"I'm going to give her a testimonial, Tanaka-san. It certainly resists." Levi bobbed his head at it. "I can't reach the controls, and I can't keep up this pace much longer. It'll drag me."

"Hold on." I ran over to the climber next to Levi and took the steps two at a time. My thighs and calves contracted from the burn. At the top, I bent over the rails, extended my arm, and stretched my fingers toward Levi's controls. "I can't quite reach."

Sweat dotted Levi's brow, wisps of hair already matted to his forehead. "See these ledges along the stairs? Straddle them and try to scale up. You can reach around me to the control panel."

I studied the ledges running up my machine. "Got it." I stepped off backward and made a mental inventory of my next steps. "On my way. Hold on—"

Thump.

Something struck me in the back of my knee, and I stumbled forward. I grabbed the rail of Levi's machine and swung my body upright.

When I'd recovered, I spotted the sandbag weight that had struck me. Trevor paced into view, holding another sandbag. He lifted it and heaved it toward my gut.

I gasped on impact and folded forward, then slumped to the ground and wedged myself between Levi's stair-climber and an elliptical.

"What's the plan, Trev?" Sweat trickled down the back of my neck. "Murder the entire town?"

Trevor raised his eyebrows. "Oh, it could have ended with Barbara Lou. But the tree-swinging mayor interrupted me."

"You're one rotten orphan, Annie!" Levi yelled.

"So, you lure us to the gym to steam us alive?" I ask. "Then what?"

"It's not super obvious? I stage everything to look like Barbara Lou did it. Then she dies too."

"Of course, your attempted murder of Marisol failed. Did you know that? She's probably blabbing to the police right now."

Trevor studied me with intensity, unable to determine whether I was telling the truth. He cracked his neck, and the corner of his lips tugged into a smirk. His mannerisms seemed familiar.

"You look just like Nick," I blurted and barked out a laugh. "Was that your plan? Become Nick? Steal his life? Live in his house? Star in his videos?"

Trevor worked his jaw. "All this snooping, and you're still completely off base. I didn't want Nick's life. He had a life he didn't deserve. I wanted to take his life away from him. Killing Nick got me justice."

"Justice?" I focused on Trevor's expression, and suddenly, the image of that little boy in the photo, being hugged by his father, gave me my second gut punch. "Your dad. He… He was also a drug addict."

"Shut your face. He was super sick. In pain. The car accident messed him up." Trevor shuffled his feet, clearly agitated. "The doctors stopped prescribing his meds. He begged them, but they wouldn't help."

I pulled myself up from the ground. "Nick sold your dad the fentanyl that caused the overdose."

"He was out of options." Trevor took a few steps backward as if pushing away.

"And he became addicted." Not only did opioid addiction happen quickly, but users developed a tolerance that required more to feel the same effects. It was a deadly vicious circle. "How did you find Nick after all this time?" I asked.

Trevor let out a laugh that sounded dark and lonely all at once. "My aunt exercised to Barbara Lou's videos. And there he was. Smiling and laughing, having a good time. My dad dies, and Nick gets this super-cool life? New identity? New teeth? New everything? And I got nothing. I don't even remember my mom, Nick killed my dad, and I spent six years with my aunt, in a place I hated. Nick *never* paid for his crimes. I made sure he did."

I looked up at Levi, who was focused on maintaining his pace. He flicked his eyes to the area behind me. I turned toward the racks of sandbag weights, kettlebells, and push bumpers. The equipment lined the wall that ran into the women's locker room. Was Levi suggesting that I escape? Or did he want me to run into the locker room and grab Barbara Lou's cell while armed with a kettlebell?

"Run, Tanaka-san!"

Without questioning Levi, I sped down the aisle of ellipticals, heading for the women's locker room. I heard Trevor stumble against the equipment as he tried to push through it and follow me.

Instead of taking a direct path to the locker room, I spun around and ran down the next aisle of cardio machines. I stopped when I reached the other side of Levi's stair-climber. I breathed deeply and hoped the machine concealed my position.

Trevor's shoes pounded into the carpet as he ran down the aisle in front of me. I slipped around the stair-climber and moved toward the locker room, turning my body sideways to maneuver through the equipment in my path.

"He's coming, Tanaka-san!"

Levi's warning gave me enough time to grab a kettlebell from the rack, twirl around, and launch it. Trevor turned to dodge it, but the kettlebell clipped his kneecap. He dropped to one knee, giving me a split second to reach behind and snatch something else—the inflatable bumper I'd used to spar with Nick.

Running full-tilt, gripping the bumper like a club, I slammed into Trevor's shoulder, and he toppled over like a bowling pin. Our momentum caused me to somersault over him before flopping onto my back.

"Sock it to him, Noodle Arms!" Levi shouted.

I limped up, clutching the bumper, but on the other side of the equipment rack. Benefiting from our position change, Trevor staggered for another sandbag weight and lobbed it at me.

I dodged the bag. "Why Celeste?" I asked between ragged breaths. "She didn't know about you. You didn't have to kill her."

"Nick would have eventually figured out who I was and told Celeste. I discovered she was Nick's sponsor, thanks to you."

"Thanks to me?"

"I followed you to the church that night. Discovered it was where all you junkies hung out. Then I heard your call to Chief Malone."

"You mean…?" I flashed to the night of the meeting, standing outside the Methodist church, debating on calling Monday or Levi.

Trevor swung the kettlebell in my direction. It shot toward me like a comet. I raised my push bumper, which—shockingly—did little to block the ten-pound chunk of cast iron.

Don't bring an inflatable bumper to a kettlebell fight.

The kettlebell bashed against my knuckles, causing considerable pain and loss of balance. I toppled to the ground, the bumper sailing from reach. Trevor hefted a massive kettlebell, which was thirty pounds at least, above his head and lurched toward me.

"This isn't justice, Trevor. It's vengeance." I crab-walked backward, bumping against some equipment. "You killed two people and put a third in the hospital."

Trevor glanced away, the kettlebell wavering as he hesitated. Then he furrowed his brow in determination and locked his eyes on me.

I pressed my palms into the ground, still trying in vain to push through whatever was blocking my path.

A red-and-black streak in the shaggy form of a Brussels griffon latched onto Trevor's ankle socks. Lulah growled as she clenched her jaw around the elastic, her back end rising from the ground.

Trevor yelped, flustered and confused by Lulah's sneak attack. He shuffled his feet to release her grip, but Lulah wasn't deterred. Twisting his upper body to look down, Trevor jerked the kettlebell he was still hefting in the air, causing him to lose his balance and topple sideways into the equipment rack.

I yanked a resistance band off a wall hanger and looped it around Trevor's wrists. He groaned as I stretched the band out and wrapped it around his ankles in a suburban equivalent of hog-tying.

"Make sure it's tight, Tanaka-san." Levi wheezed from the stair-climber. "Super, super, *super* tight."

Police sirens wailed in the distance.

Chapter 21

LEVI AND I SAT in our usual swivel chairs at the lunch counter of the Cherry Blossom.

"I can't believe Trevor stole medication from terminally ill patients." Levi's knife cracked through the breading of his *tonkatsu*, a deep-fried pork cutlet.

"Doctors often prescribe fentanyl for pain management when… well, when addiction isn't the major concern. Those patches made a convenient murder weapon." I sipped my water to soothe the burn around my lips. Jenny had pan-fried the chicken for my *yakitori* skewers before grilling them with pearl onions and cherry tomatoes. She'd Texas-fied the recipe with bacon-wrapped jalapeños.

"Our memory-care facility has a great reputation," Levi said, his mouth full of pork. "The staff doesn't just serve opioids with the pudding."

"The FDA instructs healthcare workers to flush used fentanyl patches. Trevor might have observed one of the hospice staff using a trash can instead. It happens. A kilogram of fentanyl can kill five hundred thousand people. Trevor got what he needed from a few lazily discarded patches."

Abilene had admitted the temptation to pilfer medications while her aunt lay dying in hospice. Trevor had faced a similar dilemma, chosen differently, and claimed two victims. Is controlling those impulses what separates average citizens from small-town psychopaths? I swirled a jalapeño chunk through the umami-sweet dipping sauce, ignoring the protests from my sensitive stomach.

"Trevor wanted justice," Levi said. "Killing Nick with the same drug that killed his dad qualified, I guess."

My internet research had found that a car accident had left Trevor's father with some crushed discs. Several failed operations later, his doctors prescribed fentanyl for pain management, but addiction became the more serious problem. When Trevor's father ran out of willing doctors, he used drug dealers to feed the monster. That was when Nick entered Trevor's life. Trevor had acted as an unwitting mule for his dad, even purchasing his father's final fatal dose of fentanyl from Nick.

"Chief Malone told me the aerobics shoot was Trevor's second attempt to kill Nick," Levi said. "The first time was when he found Barbara Lou at the guesthouse. Apparently, Trevor wasn't just there to deliver vape juice."

The *yakitori* in my gut flip-flopped at the mention of Monday. We hadn't spoken since the interview after I discovered Marisol.

I hadn't seen her around the café and wondered if she was avoiding me too. I wasn't sure how that made me feel. "I suppose Trevor planned to squeeze the fentanyl into Nick's water pitcher. The one he kept in the fridge." I bit into a cherry tomato, releasing its sugary juices. "Trevor offered us water at the guesthouse. Did you drink any?"

Levi cocked an eyebrow. "You don't think…?"

"He sent us to the Lone Star to steam us alive. Attempting to poison us isn't illogical."

"Adjusting his plan to murder Nick at the aerobics shoot was clever. Disturbingly so." Levi shivered but maintained his food-bites-per-minute pace. "Trevor knew the crew would be all around that studio, not to mention the temperamental talent. Certainly expanded the list of suspects."

I blotted my flaming lips with a napkin. "Don't forget Trevor played both of us. He preyed on our insecurities, trying to divide us."

"It didn't work. Not for long anyway," Levi said. "I suppose Trevor poisoned Nick's nicotine patch instead of the water bottle to deflect suspicion. If he only needed a small dose of fentanyl, how could he successfully kill Nick and Celeste, but Marisol survived?"

"Nick and Celeste were in recovery. With nothing in their systems, they had no drug tolerance." I pushed a chicken piece across my plate. "Oddly, Marisol's opioid use saved her life. The hairbrush didn't have enough fentanyl to kill her."

After a few doses of Narcan in the ER, Marisol had identified Trevor as her "party planner." Paranoid about what Nick might have shared about his past, Trevor stalked Marisol around town and used her drug abuse against her by offering a party she would never forget.

Trevor's motive for killing Marisol was murky, but she'd called him a "stalker" when he showed more knowledge of Nick's fitness career than she had. Once he learned why Nick, Celeste, and Marisol were attending church, Trevor probably misconstrued Marisol's dig as a reference to his true identity. Disposing of Marisol and planting used fentanyl patches in the nightstand Bible became another deflection tactic.

"How did Trevor get into her hotel room?" Levi hefted a forkful of pickled plum coleslaw. I celebrated his cabbage consumption as a baby step toward a more balanced diet.

"Marisol noticed her missing key after the last fitness shoot. My best guess is Trevor snagged it from her purse sometime between her finding the bag of hair and Barbara Lou's outburst over the police questioning."

"Trevor probably knew Barbara Lou was carrying around that hair, trying to test Nick's DNA. He probably figured that out after he caught her trashing the guesthouse."

That night at the Lone Star, while Levi was bound to the stair-climber, and I was dodging kettlebells, a half-naked Barbara Lou had limped through the outside door in the men's locker room and caught the attention of an on-patrol Officer Perkins.

In an interview with the *Bluebonnet Bee,* Barbara Lou said flinging herself onto the hood of a police cruiser while keeping her towel in place was the official sign she needed to retire. She also revealed her cancer diagnosis and treatment plan.

I took another drink. "With Barbara Lou retiring, I wonder what will become of the Lone Star. I should apologize to Ramona for my… aggressive questioning. Trevor must have slipped the original script through Barbara Lou's mail slot to maximize fireworks."

"That's right. The draft with the modified exercises. Vaughn wrote that after Barbara Lou's cancer diagnosis. But that paper reeked of Ramona's perfume. It could have been her."

"Everything in that gym reeked of her rose water. The essential oils from the cleaning solutions and Vaughn's cigarette stench just minimized it. Trevor printed the script from the office computer—anyone who knew Vaughn would have guessed his password—so Ramona's perfume was already on the paper."

"Don't stress about Ramona. Showbiz people have short memories." Levi set down his fork long enough to slap my back. "Vaughn's scouting his next superstars. He pitched me an idea that includes us."

"Us? As in you and me?"

"How about a best-buds aerobics video titled *Studs, Sleuthing, and Sit-Ups?*"

I blinked. "Do I need to say no, or do the facial expressions suffice?"

"It's a working title. How about *Caballeros, Crime Solving, and Cardio*? That one's Latin-inspired. We could do some of the Zumba." Levi jiggled in his swivel chair.

"I have zero interest in doing *the* Zumba. I've retired Ojii-chan's tracksuit."

Levi sighed. "Being my full-time deputy won't pay the bills. I offer loads of perks but no dental."

"For once, we agree. I need a job."

Levi froze in mid-chew. "Back to nursing?"

"The ICU can be a dark place. And death seems to have followed me to Bluebonnet Hills. If I'm not doing something I love, what's the point?"

"Looky there. Another layer of the Tanaka onion just shed itself. I knew you had a bucket list in there." The corners of Levi's mouth twitched. "So where's your next adventure?"

I chuckled. "I've always wanted to go to Mars."

"Ah, space nerd. That clocks."

"If by space nerd you mean exploring the most exciting place in our solar system. A planet with water, volcanoes, mountains, polar caps—"

"Pretty sure that's the denotation of 'space nerd.'" Jenny

stood behind the lunch counter. "You're leaving Bluebonnet Hills, Sho-chan?"

I sensed some disappointment in my sister's voice, which affirmed my decision. "I thought I'd begin my job hunt here."

She smiled. "One of your better ideas. Besides, if you're rocketing up to Mars, you'll want to focus on that stock portfolio diversification." She slid a plate of ribs toward Levi. "I experimented with my sauce. Give me your honest opinion. Be brutal. I can take it."

Jenny curled her fingers as she watched him eat. If the sauce didn't zing his taste buds, it might be Levi's last supper.

Levi balanced the bone on the plate's edge and chewed contemplatively. "I taste mirin, sugar, soy… That toasty flavor must be miso." He scratched his chin as Jenny almost leaped over the counter in anticipation. "But there's something else I can't quite identify." He clicked his tongue. "Kind of nutty."

Jenny was about to burst. "Sake!"

Levi took another bite for confirmation.

"Why the obsession with ribs?" I asked. "Is this more yes-harnessing?"

"Saying yes certainly got my adrenaline going," she said. "It also made my culinary juices pop. I can't run a Texas café without mastering barbecue. There's a local competition in a few months. If I can avoid embarrassing myself, entering it would give the Cherry Blossom some visibility."

"We'll be your official taste testers," Levi said. "You game, deputy?"

"Why not? I'll embrace the power of yes." I raised my water glass. "A barbecue competition would be an entertaining distraction from murder."

What's the worst that could happen?

Author's Notes

Thank you for taking a chance on a new writer and a new series. I have a lot more planned for Sho, Levi, Jenny, and the quirky residents of Bluebonnet Hills.

I drafted *Aerobics* early in the pandemic while caring for my newborn son. While fortunate to have extended leave from my job, I still needed to keep my brain active to focus on my child.

Since I couldn't exercise in a physical gym, I streamed fitness workouts from home. I did a lot of low-impact, high-intensity routines, as I didn't have the room or the equipment for much else. Lil Rivers sat in his carrier on the coffee table while I stumbled around the living room. It provided sufficient entertainment to both.

The concept for the Bucket List Mysteries had been rattling around in my head for a few years, but it was during one of my workouts that I merged the idea of the series with aerobics. The image of two guys dressed in cheesy, neon-colored aerobics gear made me chuckle.

I wrote the first draft in ten- to twenty-minute sprints between Lil River's naps and feedings. I also dictated in the afternoons while I pushed a stroller along the greenbelt behind our home. For me, this book is a time capsule that captures the joys of fatherhood while living in near-isolation during a global pandemic.

The pandemic doesn't exist in Bluebonnet Hills, but my stories don't shy away from serious subjects. For example, the number of fentanyl-related deaths in the US—and my state of Texas—has significantly increased over the years. As a new parent, I'm keenly aware my son will encounter situations I couldn't have fathomed.

My two protagonists, Sho Tanaka and Levi Blue, also carry some emotional baggage. My intuition was always to depict Sho as someone grappling with substance abuse, but my inner critic told me the topic was too serious for a cozy or traditional mystery. So, the early drafts of *Aerobics* tiptoed around Sho's inner conflict, making for an aimless, uninteresting read.

I'm grateful to my editor, who noted that while readers expect their cozies to have limited on-page violence, no overt sex, and minor to no profanity, it didn't mean they wanted a completely sterile reading experience.

The Bucket List Mysteries will continue to explore heavier topics but will remain lighthearted and humorous. It's a delicate balance that I take seriously, and my priority remains to entertain you.

Thanks again for reading,

—Ryan

About Ryan

Ryan Rivers is the author of the Bucket List Mystery series, featuring Levi Blue and Sho Tanaka.

By day, Ryan teaches technical writing and stops the spread of unnecessary adverbs and vague pronoun references. By mid-afternoon/early evening, he fights crime with his trusty sidekick and toddler son. Together they have uncovered who, in fact, has got your nose and tracked the elusive Peekaboo. They live and eat and occasionally sleep in North Texas with their Brussels griffon pup.

Visit Ryan at http://www.ryanriversbooks.com

Email Ryan at ryan@ryanriversbooks.com

Also By

I WRITE A LOT OF CONTENT in the Bucket List world, including novels, short stories, and novellas.

I use a simple titling system to help you find what you want.

My novels are an "alphabet mystery" series. The keyword for each title starts with the next letter of the alphabet:

Aerobics Can Be Deadly
books2read.com/aerobics

Barbecue Can Be Deadly
books2read.com/bbq

My short works are titled with a holiday:

Arbor Day Can Be Deadly
(free when you subscribe to my newsletter)
https://BookHip.com/WJSHVFN

Halloween Hoedowns Can Be Deadly
books2read.com/spooky

Note: This book includes affiliate links. This means that I receive a small percentage of sales with no extra costs to you.

www.ingramcontent.com/pod-product-compliance
Lightning Source LLC
Chambersburg PA
CBHW050850190726

48286CB00007B/2304